CHANGING LINES

Harrisburg Railers, book 1

_____

RJ SCOTT

V.L. LOCEY

Love Lane Books

Copyright

Dedication

To my big brother for agreeing to field questions from two exuberant MM authors about his home, the city of Harrisburg, and for being one dang cool older sibling throughout the years. *hugs* ~V.L. Locey

To Vicki, who gave me back the joy of writing after I thought I might lose it. And, for my family, who support my new love of hockey, and my obsession with a certain team, with long suffering sighs and gentle pats on the head. ~RJ Scott

With grateful thanks to Meredith for her beautiful cover, Rebecca for making us look good, Rachel for sorting us out, and our army of proofers for their hard work.

Changing
LINES

—— HARRISBURG RAILERS 1 ——

RJ SCOTT &
V.L. LOCEY

Love Lane Books

ONE

Tennant

"Ten, honestly, I think you should talk to your agent again."

I looked at the three faces staring at me from my laptop monitor. The one talking now was Brady, my oldest brother. Brady plays for Boston. He's their captain. He has a beautiful blonde wife named Lisa, who's a legal aide, two-year-old twin girls Gwendolyn and Amelia, and a house that you need Google maps to navigate. Brady is thirty-one and one of the best defensemen in the league. He's also the pushiest and bossiest person in the history of ever.

"I'm not talking to my agent again, Brady. It's a done deal, and I'm really sort of okay with it," I told Mr. Overachiever, and cracked open another peanut shell. The pile of empty hulls sitting beside me on the sofa was impressive.

"If he's happy, Brady, I think we should back him instead of trying to make him feel worse about it."

Face number two and the current talker was Jamie, or James as my mother always calls him. Jamie is the middle Rowe brother and plays hockey as well. He lives in Fort

Lauderdale, where he's an alternate captain and plays left wing. Jamie is also married to a Lisa—I call her Brunette-Lisa, and Brady's wife Blonde-Lisa. Not to their faces, of course, but how else am I going to differentiate? Brunette Lisa's a stunning dental hygienist who's expecting their first child in three months. They've been married for four years. Jamie's role in the Rowe-trio dynamic is Mr. Negotiator.

"There's really not much that can be done at this point anyway. His contract was only for three years, and Harrisburg picked him up." And that was talker three, my dad, Bruce Rowe. Sire of the famed Rowe brothers from South Carolina. Dad's a district manager for several Happy Marts in the Myrtle Beach and surrounding areas, and has forgotten more about hockey than the three of us players will ever know. If you look at my dad, you can see all of us in about thirty years. Black hair still thick and wavy, green-blue eyes, and a smile that Mom says still gets him into trouble.

"But really, Dad, he's taking a step back in his career," Brady said yet again.

I chewed and listened. That's my role in the family. Tennant, the baby brother, is preached to by the older Rowe boys, because obviously he has no clue what to do with his life. He *is* the youngest, after all. Mom always coddles him. Just look at him sitting there in a small apartment in Dallas, lacking a fancy house, with no sexy model with double Ds on his arm, and now being traded to some team that didn't even manage to make the playoffs last year.

"To go from an established team like Dallas to this new expansion team in Pennsylvania is a slap in the face. His agent should have pitched a fit. I mean, the very least he should have done was get him signed to an Original Six team."

4

"Oh, here we go, time to look down your nose at those of us who aren't playing for Boston or New York or Montreal," Jamie snapped.

Dad and I exhaled theatrically. I broke another shell open and Dad took a sip of his coffee. This would run on for some time.

"Jamie, don't start that shit again. I never meant there was anything wrong with playing for an expansion team," Brady said as if by rote.

"Right, like you haven't been sitting here for fifteen minutes telling Ten what a shit deal he just got being traded to an expansion team. Was that not you just saying all that in your whiny Boston accent? Get out of the way, Boof." Jamie removed his ginger cat from the laptop keyboard.

Brady was on that like white on rice. "Okay, for one thing I do *not* have a Boston accent." He really did. "But if I did, I'd be proud of it even if it was whiny. Secondly, I'm not saying that some expansion teams haven't done well for themselves over the years but…"

My mother sat down beside my dad with her own cup of coffee. She gave me a smile. I knew it was for me, because it was her special 'Tennant is my baby' smile. Mom was the exact opposite of the Rowe men: fair, blonde, and petite. She still taught music at the high school all three Rowe brothers had attended. It was Mom who'd loved hockey to death but still insisted that her boys learn to play one musical instrument so they had skills outside shooting pucks and knocking people on their asses.

"But nothing. Who won the Stanley Cup last year? Yeah, that's right, an expansion team. Suck. My. Dick."

"*James!*"

"Sorry, Mom, I didn't see you there. Boof was in the way."

"I'm sure Tennant knows what suits his life best," my mother said.

"I don't really feel bad about it," I said yet again, as I pondered easing out of the Skype group call and fading to black. My brothers and father wouldn't even notice I was gone for at least five minutes.

The conversation about me and my butchered career ran on as my mother and I made silly faces at each other. When Brady had to go give the twins their baths, Jamie remembered he had to scoop out the cat box. Dad kissed Mom on the cheek, and then padded off to watch an old western starring James Coburn.

"Well, now that the know-it-alls have left, why don't we talk?" Mom pulled the laptop across the kitchen table and leaned in close to the monitor. "How do you honestly feel about this trade, Tennant?"

I swallowed the mouthful of peanut. "It's really okay." Her thin eyebrows tangled. "No, seriously, I'm fine with it. I'm thinking this might be my chance to get out of that huge shadow Tate Collins throws over every center on the team."

"I thought you liked Tate."

I took a swig of chocolate milk and looked from the laptop on my thighs to the city of Dallas spread out below my condominium. Tate Collins *was* Dallas hockey. You know that song about the stars at night being big and bright? Well, no star shone brighter than Tate Collins in the heart of Texas. He was the face of hockey, the league's premier center, and its goal-scoring leader for three years running. No way I would ever be noticed—or have a shot at first line—with Tate on the team. And that was nothing against Tate. Tate was a good guy. Friendly, humble, generous, everything a hockey player should be. But for those who toiled away in his shadow, the darkness got depressing at times. I knew, for a fact, that I could be first line on any other team. For sure, first line on a second-year team like the Railers. That wasn't ego talking, it was confidence speaking. I knew my skill set, and it wasn't second line.

"I do, but I'm tired of being in someone's shadow all the time."

"That's the curse of being the youngest, honey." Mom gave me a sad little smile. "How's Chris going to feel about you leaving Dallas?"

The half-gallon carton of milk slipped off my lower lip. "Chris?" I coughed and hurried to wipe my chin with the back of my hand. No way. No way could she know about Chris. He and I had been super discreet.

"Yes, Christine, that bouncy redhead you took to the Texas Athlete of the Year Award over the summer?" Mom gave me a look that said she wondered about my brain. "She tweeted about it for weeks."

"Oh, Christine, right." Sure, I knew who she meant now. One of several dates who served as beards. Yep, *that* Chris, not Chris the barista with the beard and man-bun, who I'd been hooking up with on the sly for a couple of weeks. "That kind of died off."

"Oh, that's a shame. She was pretty. Anything on the horizon?"

"Nope, not really."

Dallas shimmered with heat even though it was night. The Texas Athlete of the Year Award. I recalled it well. I'd come in second to Tate for the Brightest Star on Ice award two years in a row.

"That's probably just as well. You'll be moving soon. I'm sure there are lots of lovely girls in Harrisburg."

"I'm sure there are."

Ugh, this sucked. Lying sucked. Being the only kid on either side of the family who was gay sucked. Having to date women sucked. Having to sneak men into my apartment sucked. I worked up a measly grin for her.

"You'll meet the right person, Tennant."

My dad called for her. She rolled her eyes, and I snorted.

"I swear that man can never find his glasses. How much do you want to bet they're on top of his head?"

I chuckled.

"I'd better sign off and let you rest. You're going to have a busy few weeks packing and moving. We love you, Tennant."

"Love you too, Mom."

I closed the lid of my Dell, dropped my hands over it, and stared at the city I'd be leaving behind. I'd miss Dallas. It was one hell of a great city, with amazing fans. I wasn't sure I'd miss Chris too much. Chris with the facial hair, I mean. We'd gotten into some heavy frottage, but that was about it. He was cute, but we were missing that spark you hear so much about. Probably, if I'd been staying, we'd have gone further simply because I was tired of masturbating, and that's a piss-poor reason to sleep with someone.

I guessed being traded up North had just had another check mark put in the 'This might be an okay thing after all' column. I had a few concerns, such as finding a place to live, what the guys and coaching staff would be like, and had Frank Sinatra or any other big name ever sung any songs about Harrisburg. You know a town has made it when it has a popular song about it. Places like New York, Dallas, San Francisco, Chicago… they all had songs. Hell, even Allentown had a song. A song meant you were a kickass place to live, right? A quick Google search informed me that one dude named Josh Ritter had indeed sung about the town I was moving to. I guessed we were golden, then.

SEPTEMBER. Man... Where the hell had summer gone? Oh yeah, it had been swallowed up by searching for a new condo, packing, visiting the folks, and making sure my address was changed at the post office.

The first thing I'd noticed, as I crossed the Pennsylvania border with the last of my personal belongings in the back of my Jeep Wrangler, had been the lack of palm trees. No, seriously. Like, I'd known logically that there would be no palm trees, but actually not seeing any had been a jolt. There were lots of other trees, but nothing with a palm frond. Which meant winter was a part of life here. That was uncool. A beach baby like me and temps under forty did not play well—not at all. A checkmark under 'This might *not* be an okay thing after all' was mentally made.

Thankfully, my aunt was a realtor and had scored me one hell of a nice midtown condo on Front Street with a view of the Susquehanna River from a rooftop deck. The building was massive, brick, and was filled with "grace and charm", to quote my aunt. I'd picked up a two-bedroom unit for the same cost as my one-bedroom back in Dallas. Overall, I was happy with the place and had plans to turn the second bedroom into a gym. My furniture had arrived the day after I had, and it looked stupid. The western motif had worked back in Big D. Here in Harrisburg, it looked moronic. I'd sold off the old stuff within a week and was now working on filling the big, empty rooms with furnishings that said I was one successful urbanite. So far, I had a recliner and a bed. Oh, and the TV and my PS4. The essentials were covered, at least.

Entering the kitchen, I flipped on a light, then made breakfast, which consisted of a protein shake and a mushroom and cheese omelet. Mom and Dad had been up over the weekend, and she had filled the freezer and every shelf of the fridge with good food, aka healthy food. The six-pack had gotten a dark look, but she hadn't told me about how fattening it was or how stupid I acted with two beers under my belt. This time. Like I didn't know I had zero tolerance for alcohol?

As I ate, I scanned the local news apps on my phone. Every single one had something to say about the Railers. Most centered on the argument that the state could not support three pro hockey teams. Which was maybe right—time would tell. Hockey was growing in popularity, but it had a long way to go to catch up with football, baseball, or basketball here in the States. There were a few articles about me and the hopes the sports beat writers had for the team's offense now that they had a top six center. Scoring had been an issue last season, as had a weak defense. It would take time to build a good roster; the expansion draft only did so much for the team. The alarm on my phone went off as I was tossing my dirty plate into the dishwasher. My stomach knotted up.

Training camp for the experienced guys like me started today. The rookies on the team had been required to show up yesterday. Today would be all about medicals, fitness testing, and media. The press would be all over me like chocolate on a Ring Ding. Which was kind of cool. It would probably feel good to get some of that spotlight that had always used to shine on Tate. Hell, even growing up I was always hearing, "Oh, you're Brady/Jamie's little brother! I hope you're half the student/player he/they are!" from teachers and coaches. This was my time now, and I was going to bask in the limelight until I was burned.

A quick shower, and I was off to the training facility out in Rutherford, about twenty minutes from my condo.

Glass Animals supplied the ride-to-work music. Pulling into the parking lot of the East River Arena, home of the Harrisburg Railers Hockey team and seeing press vans scattered around filled me with nervous excitement. I slipped inside without being noticed, the crush of reporters only getting a peek at me when I jogged down a flight of steps to check out the ice. I closed my eyes, inhaled the smell of hockey into my lungs, and smiled. There was nothing like it. The cold air, the sound of blades on ice, the grunts and shouts, the impact of man against glass and board, and the flash of the goal light. It was as good as sex. The ice looked perfect. Pity we veterans wouldn't be on it until tomorrow.

"Tennant! Hey, welcome to Harrisburg! What do you think you'll bring to the team?"

I looked over the shoulder of my brand new Railers hoodie at the lean guy hustling down the concrete stairs. He had wild brown hair and big googly eyes. He held his hand out, shook, then glanced at the cell phone in his hand.

"Bob Riggs," he said. "I run an online site that deals exclusively with ice hockey in the Harrisburg area. From the pros to peewee."

"Nice. Feel free to tape."

I leaned against the glass, folded my arms over my chest, and began answering questions. Within five minutes there were probably twenty people gathered around me at ice level. I did my best to answer every question they threw at me. I told them how excited I was to be there, how I hoped I could contribute to the team and the city in a positive way, and how cool it was that professional hockey was expanding. It was an impromptu kind of meet-and-greet, my favorite kind. I related much better to this kind of setting, as opposed to the strictly regulated media day things the teams always set up. Those always felt so staged and stiff. I was about to reply to a question from a burly dude in a tracksuit who had no hair on his head but had massive amounts of it growing out of his ears, when someone pounded on the glass behind me.

I jumped and spun, my gaze locking with and then getting lost in the most beautiful light blue eyes I had ever seen. Familiar eyes, too, now that the shock began to pass. They belonged to Jared Madsen, or "Mads" as he was known in our house. I hadn't seen him in years. He looked so different, and yet the same, if that made any sense. He was incredibly hot now. Had he always been that way? I'd been probably ten or maybe twelve when I'd last seen him, so I totally hadn't been aware of men, or how attracted to them I would be a few years later. Had his hair always been that shade of golden wheat, his eyes that piercing, his shoulders that broad…?

TWO

Mads

T en stared right at me with a look of recognition and even a hint of a smile. He was gorgeous—there was no getting away from that. From his chiseled cheekbones to his green eyes, he was a step away from pretty. My reaction to him was visceral. He was exactly the kind of man I liked to spend time looking at.

Tennant Rowe. On one hand, star center and a team player with excellent hockey sense, and on the other, gorgeous, sexy, and fodder for a million fan fantasies.

I need to focus on the hockey. I have nine years on him, and he's a family friend. I decided to repeat that until I'd settled down the appreciation that had filtered into my thoughts. So, I focused on the hockey.

Even at eleven or twelve, whatever he'd been when we'd last met, it had been obvious that Tennant had the Rowe hockey genes—the potential to be better than his brothers, even. Not that Brady or Jamie had ever let him be better. Brotherly love had not extended to letting Ten get goals on them, or hell, even get the extra potato at dinner. Their competitiveness would have stifled a lesser kid, but not Ten—he'd thrived on it.

"What do you know about Tennant Rowe?" Head Coach Mike Benning had asked me before the trade. "You played with Brady, right?"

I'd almost felt like my opinion mattered right then, as if my having prior knowledge of Ten's brother Brady meant that when I spoke, Coach would actually listen. Not that he didn't listen, don't get me wrong—he was a good guy underneath the stern-faced iciness. He was just really focused on the forwards. It was one of the things the team was fucking up, not that I was saying that out loud just yet. I had camp to get through yet, finding a core of D-men I could shape. Then I'd be saying exactly what I thought to Coach Benning, and he could like it or not.

It would be too late to get rid of me then.

So yeah, he was right. I'd played with Brady in Juniors, part of the D-pair with him, and we'd been good. More than good. He'd ended up first pick to Boston, and made it to captain so damn quick it had taken even me by surprise. Then again, he'd always been a pushy bastard who'd gone after what he wanted. Me? My rise hadn't been so fast, but I'd stood out at the Buffalo Sabres, done my part in getting us to the Stanley Cup finals. Only my career was over, and Brady's star was still shining. Go figure.

"You can't judge Tennant by his brother," I'd said, and I'd meant it. Brady was a defenseman; big and ugly in the corners, with a spark that made him the best. Yeah, he was captain, yeah, he had some two-way skills, but he was no kind of forward like Ten, who had all the best top six attributes, like speed and puck smarts.

Ten was still staring, and I guessed that meant I was staring back. I sketched a small wave, and he copied me, then one of the reporters asked him something and he was distracted away from me. That was okay; wasn't like we had anything to say except that small acknowledgment of familiarity. I'd checked him out on Google when Coach had asked me, seen the standard NHL photos. One, in particular, had caught my eye. Ten in Dallas colors, stick behind his neck, smiling, his lips in a pout, eyes bright. He'd sure grown up all kinds of sexy, but given the number of photos of him and various female models, he was the wrong kind of sexy for me.

Anyway, let's face it, Brady would kill me if I went anywhere near his brother. After all, he'd walked in on the threesome thing in Montreal and been faced with me, a busty brunette, and this built-like-a-brick-outhouse guy, both of whom had been... Well, yeah, Brady had sworn he needed eye bleach, since then his opinion of me had placed me firmly in the region of whore.

Pretty accurate for the most part, at least until game five of round three, when I'd had an argument with the boards that had taken me out of a playoff game and then out of professional hockey altogether. Nothing like having your body let you down to stop your whoring ways.

I pulled myself out of thinking about Ten and his brothers when Coach Benning skated up to me.

"And?" he asked under his breath.

"And what?"

"The kid look good to you?"

"Who?"

"Tennant Rowe," he said with a hint of impatience, like I was stupid.

I could wax lyrical about the lithe body in the obvi-ously brand-new Railers hoodie, or the way his green eyes sparkled in the bright rink lights. Hell, I could even talk about how broad his back had seemed pressed up against the glass before he turned. But that wasn't what Coach was after; he wanted some instant insight into talent.

I had so much I wanted to say at that point. Something along the lines of the Railers being lucky to have someone with his stats, that the kid was a man now, who had the potential to lead the team into a good year. Maybe even playoffs. I was desperate to say that Coach shouldn't fuck it up. I didn't say a word. My shrug was the way I'd started talking to the man who couldn't tell a good player from a bad one.

Benning muttered something that sounded distinctly like it included the words "asshole" and "fuck." I was used to that now. We had what the team liked to call an interesting relationship. I called it a fucked-up mess, but I knew it wasn't all him.

A flurry of cursing and laughter, and the ten rookies I had with me that day were out on the ice. I looked at them objectively as they stretched and skated lazy circles to warm up. We had six spots on the team, four of which were already filled by some of the best D-men I'd seen in a long time. Which left spots for two out of the ten who were there for training. I already had my eye on Travis MacAllister. He'd spent last year on the minor team that fed the Railers, shown promise, been called up a couple of times but not dressed for the game. Mac, as he was known, was so close to making the team proper, and he knew it, cocky son of a bitch. I liked that in a defenseman—confidence in his abilities, that he could push anyone into the boards and walk away smiling.

I put him with this new kid—bright eyed, ruling-the-world kind of confidence radiating from every pore. He was a six-five Swede with a goofy, big-toothed smile, and appeared inoffensive at first look, but Arvid "Arvy" Ulfsson was anything but harmless. He had potential behind that smile and spent a lot of time at the net, scrappy and relentless. His weakness was his desperate need to get in on the attack, and he needed to settle his position with his mark before he got all fancy and tried to take shots at the net.

The rest were a mix of guys who shone and some who didn't. All of them deserved a place on the minor team, but whether they'd stand up well as part of the Railers was another matter.

I partnered Arvy and Mac in the three-on-two, switched them out, concentrated really hard on the edge work, on the checks they followed through, on the ones they didn't… or as hard as I could when Ten was sitting and watching.

I wonder what Ten thinks? Is he taking mental notes like me? He'd grown up practicing against his brothers, both NHL stars in their own right. Was he watching this scrimmage and thinking that the defense could be better? Was he judging Arvy and Mac? *Is he judging me? Why do I care?*

By the end of the practice, I'd mentally crossed five of the guys off the list. Telling them that they weren't being offered contracts was hard, but they had to learn, right? The NHL was the shining target, the Stanley Cup, the original six, a hundred years of history. Not everyone was guaranteed a seat at the table their first year out. One of them, a hulking bulk of a guy, seemed to want to say something, but I stood my ground, like only the best kind of enforcer could, and he subsided with a rueful grin. I couldn't blame any of the guys for their disappointment— enforcers were pushy and ultra-confident by trade, and you couldn't expect them to switch it off as soon as practice ended.

By the end of session one, I had five left, and the uneasy feeling that Ten was staring at my every move. I excused it as being because I was familiar to him, a family friend, someone he used to shoot against as a teenager on the odd occasions I would stay at the Rowe house and we'd play pick up hockey. When I casually skated a loop to bring myself up against the goalie coach, I glanced up at the seats where Ten and the rest had been sitting, but there was only empty space. They'd left, and for a second I was disappointed. I'd kind of hoped to have a chat with him afterward. What about, I didn't know.

The last thing you did was ask Tennant Rowe how his brothers were, or make a comment about the most recent Brady/Jamie success. Not that he wasn't proud, I was sure —they were a close family, and one I had envied as an only kid with an absent mother, but still… Ten had spent a long time making his own name.

I knew that, because I'd followed him. Not like a stalker, or with a Google alert set up or anything like that. I mean, I'd listened for the scraps of information out of Dallas, the mentions of Ten often as an addendum to what the great Tate Collins, Savior of the NHL, was doing. I'd seen photos of skinny Ten growing up, holding that Dallas second line with a tenacity that had got him an eighty-nine points average over the three years. I'd seen interviews after games where the reporters had wanted to ask Ten questions about his brothers. He always smiled at those, and answered as best he could, but anyone who knew him could see the frustration in his expression.

"You looking at Arvy and Mac?" Alain Gagnon, goalie coach extraordinaire, a twenty-year veteran from the Canucks, interrupted my thought process. *Arvy. Mac. Work.*

"Yeah."

Gagnon huffed. "Mac's a definite. Arvy doesn't finish his checks and wants to score goals."

"Nothing wrong with a two-way defenseman," I said. I

was aiming for sarcastic, but actually it was nice to have validation from someone I respected that things weren't quite right with Arvy.

"He's good, has potential there. So, you'll work with him," Gagnon said, and skated off.

He did that a lot. The skating off thing. Goalies are just weird, if you ask me—funny, talking to their posts kind of weird. But then, if you're the type of man who's happy standing still with a puck heading for you at a hundred miles an hour, you're a long way past weird. The Railers weren't looking for a new goalie this year—the two we had were what kept us from falling to the bottom of the tables. In fact, they and a few of our more sparky forwards were the ones who'd left us only eight points away from a play-offs place in the first year since expansion.

"My office," Coach called, and I skated slowly toward the door.

Part of me didn't want to leave the ice. This was my home. I felt good on the ice. Everything was soft and smooth and cold, not jagged and ruined like my life outside. And yeah, I'm aware that sounds dramatic, but the ice was, and will always be, my refuge. That first jarring step when skate hits the rubber of the walkway, you feel the entire weight of your body on that tiny blade and everything is wrong for the shortest of seconds. I didn't know if any other skaters felt that way—I'd never asked them, limited as I was mostly to being fierce and chirping the guys I was shadowing. I could just imagine it—up against an elite center, checking them into the boards and then asking them how they felt about the ice.

Not happening.

The meeting was shorter than normal, thank fuck—Benning had a way of talking until he was blue in the face and the rest of the room was losing the will to stay awake.

He was all team dynamics, pressure points, forecheck, backcheck, Xs and Os. I was all "Let's get lunch, because breakfast was a mess and I didn't manage more than one bite of a cold Pop-Tart." Apparently, the meeting was short because he had a very important, official meeting with the new forward, Tennant Rowe, shining star, part of the Rowe dynasty, and so on. He was looking at me the whole time he said that, and I think he was probably trying to say without words that even though I knew Ten, he was in charge. Who knows.

I share an office with Gagnon, but that's okay, because he's never in there. Probably off doing goalie-type weird stuff. That meant I got a chance to eat in peace, get a coffee, and scroll through my inbox. The email from Brady was expected. Not that we email a lot—hardly at all since the accident that ended my career with brutal finality. I placed my hand on my chest, a habit I had when I was thinking about my heart. One hit into the boards, one normal concussion protocol, and then I'd collapsed in the medical bay.

The beginning of the end.

Brady had been one of the first people I'd pushed away. The fucker had tried contacting me for the longest time out of all my friends, but finally even he'd given up.

Like I'd wanted friends still playing hockey when my heart condition wouldn't even allow me to play in a beer league.

Hey, Mads, the email began, and I must admit I liked that it wasn't formal. I'd been Mads since I'd started hockey at age four. Turned out having the surname Madsen *and* being described as a mad enforcer meant my nickname was a good one.

The email asked after me, hoped I was okay and liking my new role with the Railers, and said how pissed he was that Boston hadn't taken me on as a coach. Where he'd got the idea that I'd ever want to coach at Boston, I didn't know. The two of us together would just have been too much of a reminder of everything that had gone to shit.

Yep. That's me being dramatic again.

I read the rest. Some news about his twins, and the fact that he was about to be an uncle. For a moment my chest tightened. Ten was way too young to be a dad, and I should know—I'd been only just fifteen when I'd helped create a kid. Why I immediately assumed it was Ten who'd done the deed I don't know, given that there was Jamie, the middle brother.

And then the email cut to the chase. *So you know you're getting Ten—keep an eye on him for me? The team isn't what I wanted for him, but he's set on this.*

Then there was the usual "we must keep in touch" crap. But I felt in the space of a sentence, the Railers had been dismissed as worthless. I'd been told that Ten was better than us, and I'd been demoted to the role of care-taker. Somehow all that gelled together to make me feel like shit.

I typed out a response that was flowery with adjectives, cast aspersions on Brady's parentage, and told him in no uncertain terms to shove his platitudes where the sun didn't shine.

I then deleted it all and just sent a simple, *He's all grown up—he can look after himself.* I hesitated over what to sign it. Mads was the right way to go, but somehow it implied a personal connection that I didn't feel happy with. But Brady had never called me Jared, so in the end I wrote Mads and pressed send.

The whole thing left me as unsettled as I felt with my skates on rubber, and I shut my email down, deciding later would be a good time to tackle the emails from Ryker's school, the bank, and the amendments to the myriad schedules that ruled a hockey team.

Coffee in hand and restless, I left my office, bypassing the changing rooms, the kitchen, the weight rooms, and in fact any place where I might meet someone and have to talk. Which was how I ended up in the back corridor by the heap of storage boxes we used when playing away games. Unfortunately, someone else was already there, seated on a box, cross-legged, staring at the wall. Tennant. I stopped and backed away, but he'd heard me, or seen me, or really did have that freaky second sight that some of the pundits talked about.

"Mads," he said, and leaned forward out of the shadows so I was able to get a good look at him. The dark blue hoodie with the Railers logo front and center suited him. That was all I could think.

"Ten," I said, on autopilot.

"That guy, twenty-nine. Ulffson or something? He's not finishing his checks. Wants to get the puck and score. That's not good."

I looked at Ten to see if he was teasing, but there was nothing on his face or in his beautiful green eyes that spoke of the declaration being anything other than a statement of fact.

"Noted," I said.

"You knew that already," Ten said, and untangled his legs, stretching them out in front of him one at a time.

"I did."

Great, this was either the deepest conversation I'd ever had with another person, or just plain fucking stupid.

"Brady says hi," Ten offered, and this time the stretching extended to him lifting his arms above his head, and yep, there it was, that strip of skin, of toned stomach, and yep, I looked. Sue me, Ten had a classic skater's body, all muscles and planes and strength. A man could look.

And then I raised my gaze, and Ten was smirking. Honest-to-God smirking at me. What did that mean? Was it because he knew he looked good and he was appreciating the fact that someone had looked? Or was it because Brady had told Ten about the threesome incident and he was hoping to push my buttons? Either way, Ten was a bastard who was happy flaunting all his shit, and I couldn't be interested. I should just come out with it and call him on the smirk, tell him I might be bi but I wouldn't be fucked around with. But what if the smirk was because of something else, like a family joke that was about me?

So, I didn't say a thing. I changed the subject and chalked up the reason for the smirk as nothing at all.

"Great. He actually emailed me," I said, referring back to Brady, because I wasn't going to smile back or rise to anything Ten was implying with that smirk.

At that statement, Ten's expression changed. From confident and happy, he became guarded. "Don't tell me," he began with a heavy sigh. "Big Brother wanted to warn you that I need to try harder on the breakaway, or that my forecheck isn't as fast as we need, or hell, maybe I'm not in the right place for the tip in."

"No," I answered, because the words Ten spoke were filled with derision, and I didn't like him saying any of it. "Your brother is proud of you."

All the tension left Ten, and he visibly slumped. "Yeah, I know he is. I'm proud of him *and* Jamie." He looked right at me. "Don't think for one minute we're not one big *happy* family."

Ouch. Something really hard underscored those words, and I wanted to fix whatever had stolen away happy, teasing Ten and left this shuttered man in front of me.

"He wanted to meet up one day for a beer," I lied. Because whatever I tell my son about lying not being a good thing, lying is sometimes exactly what needs to happen.

"Oh." Ten looked surprised. Then he smiled again, this time less confident smirk and more fond. "How's Ryker?"

"Seventeen, hormonal, a pretty good left wing." That was how I summed Ryker up in public. But Ryker was much more than my moody seventeen-year-old son who had a wicked slap shot. He was my life, and the reason I got up every day.

When I'd sat in that doctor's office and listened, hearing words that meant very little to me, I'd interrupted him and asked him the one thing any hockey player would ask. Will I play again?

Only having my son in my life had stopped me from losing myself in pills and alcohol after the doctor had shaken his head and put the final nail in my hockey coffin.

You won't be able to play professional hockey again.

So, yeah, Ryker was more than how I'd described him there, but I wasn't ready to share that with anyone, let alone Ten, who I didn't really know very well anymore.

"I friended him on Facebook," Ten announced.

I wasn't even Ryker's Facebook friend. I needed to talk to him about that, because I should be, right? Isn't that, like, number one on the list for parental responsibility or something? It was my turn to have him this weekend, and I added Facebook to my mental list of things to talk about.

"Good," I finally answered. Probably with too much of a gap for it to be socially acceptable. Whatever I did wrong was enough for Ten to clamber off the crate and straighten up. He held out his hand.

"I'm going to like it here," he said.

I took his hand. A man's hand now. Not the same grip he'd had as a kid. I shook it firmly, and he had that same smile. Was I supposed to hug him now? Was that what a "bro" would do? He tugged away and slipped past me.

"Later," he said.

And all I could think was that Ten had surely grown up fine.

THREE

Tennant
————————

I was firing off a text to Brady as soon as I rounded the corner, leaving Mr. Jared "Sultry Blue Eyes" Madsen behind. It was short and to the point.

Stay the fuck out of my life.

I hit send. Then thought of something else to tell Brady.

I mean it. No more emails to Mads. EVER. About anything regarding me.

I glanced up, danced around a dude I assumed was an equipment manager, given the skates dangling over both shoulders, then sent off text three to make sure my older brother really got it. Sometimes he didn't. Like, all the time he didn't.

Seriously. No more. I'll tell Mom.

I paused, staring at the text, then erased the part about Mom. That was my ace in the hole. Didn't want to play it too soon.

Seriously. No more. It's my life. Stop trying to run it. U suck.

There. That sounded good. Should I send him the smiling pile of shit emoji just to drive home what I thought he was? Walking and texting. Probably dangerous. Okay, totally dangerous. A soccer ball bounced off my skull. I dropped my phone and yelped.

A voice broke into my pain. "Bouncing big balls," it announced.

I crouched down to pick up my phone, then stood, my gaze traveling up and up and up to reach the face of the man who'd been kicking the ball off the concrete walls. The tone of the words, heavily accented, conveyed apology.

"It's cool," I said immediately. "My mother always says that texting and walking will be the death of me." I pocketed my cell and held out my hand. "Tennant Rowe."

The behemoth took my hand and shook. "Stanislav Lyamin. Stan."

"Right. I watched your tapes."

The dude was *huge*. It was like shaking hands with Groot. He topped out at six nine or ten easily, and probably weighed two fifty if not more. His hair was dark and buzzed to his scalp. He had stormy gray eyes and a long, aristocratic nose. The Railers had picked him up from the KHL for a song. Stan had size and grit in spades. He filled the net, but lacked speed and agility. Once they trimmed him down a bit, he'd move faster and seal that net up tight.

"You like soccer, huh?" I asked.

"Silly rabbit."

I gaped dully at the big man. "Oh-kay, yeah. Well, I was just heading off to dinner, so…"

"Big Mac."

Stan rubbed his belly and then followed me for a few steps. I stopped walking and looked up at him. He stared down at me. Shit, but the man was intimidating. Glad I didn't have to go up against him.

"Yeah, right, food, so… I'm leaving to go eat." I waved

at the nearest exit and smiled broadly, inching away from the tender. "Nice to meet you."

"I am a Pepper."

"Dude, are you saying you want to hit Mickey D's or something?" I looked around for someone—anyone—to save me, but it was just me and the Russian in shorts and sneakers.

"They're *great!*"

"Stan, you have been watching *way* too much American TV," I chuckled.

Twenty minutes later, we were shoving burgers and fries into our faces while drawing all kinds of odd looks. It had to be Stan pulling all the gawks. He kind of stood out, but he was funny. His gray eyes never settled. Like never. They darted around constantly. I wondered if he was just working on tracking exercises while he ate. I'd seen a video of the goalie down in D.C. doing the same thing in preparation for a game. Although, since we weren't getting ready to play, maybe he was just trying to absorb all this America.

"Lip-smacking good," he said after polishing off his fourth burger. I'd made do with one and some fries. Empty calories. Not on my healthy eating plan, but man was the grease tasty.

"It sure is. Okay, so here's the thing. I'm new to this town. Like, I don't know anyone." I sat back and took a sip of my milkshake. Man, I'd be running to Chicago tomorrow to work off this meal. "Well, I mean, I know Mads, but he's like this weird thing, right?"

Stan's smoky eyes landed on me and stayed glued there. My gaze roamed over the menu above the cashiers' heads.

"Weird like he's so much sexier than I remembered."

I drifted a bit, the prices getting blurry as I pulled up

an image of the Railers defensive coach in my mind. Fuck, but he was hot. Those sky-blue eyes and that mouth… He smelled good too. His cologne was brisk, kind of nautical. A kid a couple of booths over screamed, jarring me from the memory of his hand in mine. Mads had a strong grip.

"Shit, uh, yeah, so I know no one here aside from Mads and his grip." Stan watched me, and I sought some kind of common ground we could talk about that wasn't hockey. My cell chimed to let me know I had a notification on my Pokémon game. "You ever play games on your phone?" I shook the phone. "Pokémon?"

He chewed and stared. I opened up my current game and waved it under his nose. He shrugged and then his eyes lit up. "Pikachu," he announced. Seems like Pokémon was a cross-borders kind of thing.

"Okay, well, I think we should start our own academy for Pokémon trainers on the team." I showed him the screen again.

He nodded while sucking down half a super-sized Coke. I kid you not. One huge pull and half the soda gone. It was incredible.

"It'll be like this bonding thing, right?"

Stan smiled.

"Cool! So, you're in then?"

Some lady ran past chasing a ketchup-coated toddler. Stan kept smiling as he opened the first of five tiny apple pies stacked on his tray.

"We should have a team name. I mean besides the Railers, although I guess that would work."

"Tumbling minions."

"Yep, for sure. Hey! You know what we could do now?"

Stan took a bite of his pie and shook his buzzed head.

"I want to go find an ink shop and get my favorite

Pokémon. Do you have any tattoos?" I pointed at my arm, and then his.

He frowned and then pulled back the sleeve of his jersey, exposing some pretty fucking sweet Cyrillic. I wondered what it said, but guessed I wouldn't be getting much of an explanation from Stan.

I held up my hand for a high five and got one that nearly dislocated my shoulder. Life in Harrisburg was picking up. I had a new team to bedazzle, a tall buddy who was easy to talk to, and a secret little crush on my older brother's friend. That night, I also had a brand-new tattoo on the back of my neck and a string of texts from Brady. Each one was him talking down to me, so each reply from me was the smiling pile of shit emoji. Finally, Brady sent me his last text for the night.

Grow the fuck up.

I carried a smirk with me all the way to Rutherford and the practice facility the following morning. Stan met me at the player's entrance, ducking until he was nearly bent in half to clear the doorframe. We exchanged a meaty knuckle bump.

"How's the ink?" I asked, pointing to the biceps that carried his new tat of Pikachu. I don't know why he decided to get that done, but he had been so excited. Even though I explained that this wasn't something that the team had to have to be considered 'team'.

"Po-Kee-Mon rocks." His face split into a grin.

I threw back my head and laughed. "Damn straight," I replied, and slapped his broad back.

We entered the dressing room, and I took a second to scope it out. The Railers logo stood out on the dark blue rug in the center of the semi-circular room. Everyone was careful not to step on it. Doing so was sacrilegious, and would bring down the nastiest juju on the team.

I eyed the logo critically. The old style steam train was in gray on the dusky-blue background, an echo back to the time when Harrisburg was the center for rail track production. I thought it was pretty badass actually; better than some random animal or bird. The room was packed with players, most just now stripping off their suits and gearing up for our first day as a team.

"Hey, Tennant, I didn't get to introduce myself yesterday. Media day this year was beyond crazy, then my wife insisted I hit the kids' parent-teacher conference, since I'll be scarce from here on out. Connor Hurleigh, captain of the Railers."

I shook hands with the older man. Connor was mid-thirties and had always been a damn fine center. Was he as good as me? We'd see, since he played on the first line and I wanted that spot bad. He'd come to the team last year in the expansion draft, and because of his years of experience on the ice, the team had chosen him to wear the "C" on his sweater. Rumor was he was a fine captain, if not the most demonstrative in the locker room. A lead by example kind of guy.

"It was crazy for sure," I said, then released his big hand. He was a normal-looking man. Brown hair and brown eyes. Wicked scar on his chin from a skate blade back when he played for Arizona. "I'm hoping to be able to really contribute to the team."

"That's what we like to hear."

Connor moved off to talk to some of the older players. Stan had wandered off to the corner, where he now stood staring at the cinderblocks. No one would touch or bother him. It was goalie shit. Zoning in or something. Hell, maybe that was how all Russian tendies started the routine of mental prep. What did I know? I threw myself into a meet and greet with the rest of the team, picking out the guys under thirty and inviting them to join the Pokémon fun. By the time I sat down to remove my dress shoes, I had ten guys added to the roster. Stan was still in the corner doing his oddball goalie stuff. Knowing it was time to hit the ice and make this team mine fired me up. I changed quickly and was taping my socks to help secure the shin pads when I paused and looked at the dressing room door.

This is going to sound stupid, but I sensed the coaching staff entering the dressing room way before they arrived. It was like fingerlings of static electricity snaked out ahead of Mads stepping into the room and ran up my arms, prickling the hairs at the tender nape of my neck. His gaze flickered to me. I met his look. He glanced away quickly. I sat there, half-naked, brand new yellow Railers training sweater draped over the bench beside me, staring at his profile while Coach Benning gave us the usual speech about teamwork, dedication, diligence, and so on.

We had a short video presentation, followed by the coaches splitting apart to talk to the men under them. Goalie coaches with goalies, defensive coach with the D-men, and we forwards got to listen to Associate Coach Colin Pike laying out what the organization wanted from us over the upcoming season. Like we needed to be told? Every hockey player has one goal, and that's to hoist the Cup over his head. Everything we do from the time we first lace up those tiny skates as kids is geared toward reaching that goal. We all dream the same dream. So, sure, I got it that the coaches were all about the pep talks, but I for one didn't need them. And if anyone on this team didn't have that goal as his number one priority, his ass needed to be sent off to the ECHL or something. I was done with coming in second.

We were split into four groups for this first session on

the ice. Part one of the testing was skating from goal line to goal line at top speed for three minutes straight. No stopping. We wore straps under our sweaters next to our chests to measure heart rate, breathing frequency, body temperature, acceleration and deceleration. This was all done to see where we could improve our performance. I was part of the second group. Coach Madsen and Coach Pike were running the show. The head coach was reading the information as it fed into his laptop over at the timekeeper's table.

"On my mark," Mads shouted, his voice echoing off the steel girders of the training rink. I bent down slightly, stick on the ice, and set my sights on the far end of the rink. The sharp trill of a whistle, and the four of us were off. The trick was to power into a good lead before you were tanked, because three minutes on ice is a killer. It doesn't sound like a long time, but hockey is about quick bursts of speed. Typical TOI, or time on ice, is forty-five to sixty seconds for forwards. Defensemen can go longer, but it varies per player or depending on the situation. That's why a good team rolls four solid lines one after the other. It gives us time to catch our breath and rehydrate.

I hit the goal line first, spraying ice, and spun. Both coaches on the ice were shouting encouragement to the men skating. Four times back and forth had us all winded, legs and lungs burning. Mads and Pike continued yelling at us, pushing us to keep going. When the whistle to stop finally came, my thighs and calves felt like pudding. I was sucking air like a Hoover, and sweat ran into my eyes and down the crack of my ass, but I had smoked the three others in my group, one being our captain.

"Good job," Mads said as I passed.

I gave him a nod, since speaking was not happening quite yet. I felt his gaze on me as I hit the boards in front of the home bench and draped the upper half of my body over them.

"That… sucked," I gasped to the guys waiting to take their turn.

Ten minutes later, the four of us who had the fastest times were back out for another three minutes of hell. Yay. Playing hockey was so much fun. It was close, but I eked past Troy Hanson, the first line left-winger. He was smaller than me, and lighter, but I managed to smoke him by a full two-tenths of a second. Then, after we caught our breath, it was more testing. Forty-meter sprints forward and backward, slalom pylon tests, and another round of endurance laps. When my skates hit rubber, I was spent. There was not one little puff of energy for me to pull up from deep within.

I desperately wanted some chocolate milk. I wobbled down the hall outside the Railers dressing room and rounded a corner to find Mads trying to feed a dollar bill into the coffee machine. He glanced over his shoulder. Our gazes met and held. The machine spat his buck back out, and he cussed as he bent over to pick it up.

"Need a little zip?" I asked as I padded up to the cold drinks machine.

"Something like that." He turned the bill around and tried again.

"Got a buck I can borrow?"

Mads looked at me as if I'd asked him to loan me a kidney.

I patted the back of my sweaty hockey pants. "No wallet on me."

"Oh, sure. Here, use this one. Maybe that machine will like it better."

"Thanks."

I took the wrinkled bill and tried flattening it on the

side of the soda machine. Mads dug into his wallet and pulled out a less tattered bill.

"So, what did you think of the runs?" I asked to make conversation. Standing beside him, his elbow bumping mine, and not talking seemed weird and awkward.

"You know I can't discuss that with you," he replied, then smiled as the machine sucked his buck in.

Man, that smile… it changed him. The fine lines around his eyes and mouth deepened a little. It made him look a little more mature and ten times hotter. My body tingled, a rush of desire igniting in my belly and spreading out like one of those controlled burns the forest service does. If I touched him now in some flirty way, that contained blaze would roar to life and engulf me as if I were dry tinder. Mads glanced at me when the stifling silence went on.

"Oh, yeah, uh, no, I mean, that's not what I was asking," I stammered as my exhausted body dredged up enough energy to heat my cheeks and plump up my dick a bit.

"Well, good. You did well, but you already knew that." He slapped me playfully on the back of my sweaty neck.

I winced and hissed.

"Did you injure yourself during testing?"

"Nah, it's just new ink work."

"Oh, so you got a new tattoo." He stared at me oddly.

"Yeah, Stan and I went last night and got them. It's my favorite Pokémon. Want to see?" I turned around and let my chin rest on my chest.

"It's a pony," he said. "With flippers and rubies in its mane and tail," Mads stated so dryly it was a wonder his comment didn't blow away like talcum powder.

"No, it's not *just* a pony." I spun to face him. His expression said he found my tattoo humorous. "It's

Ampharos, which is Mareep's most highly evolved form. This 'pony' will kick your ass to the Capitol building and back. I've been training a beast like it for ages."

"And this is what you do in your spare time? Evolve cartoon animals?"

Wow, he'd sounded just like the big brother I was pissed at right there.

"Just FYI—Pokémon is huge on college campuses. I also do some fantasy hockey, play video games, watch RWBY and *Doctor Who*, and read comics. Oh, and jerk off."

I arched a brow. My carton of chocolate milk dropped to the bottom of the machine. Mads stood staring at me like I'd spoken in a foreign language. I doubted he would know that RWBY was a very popular anime, but he had to know who Doctor Who was, right? The shouts and laughter from the dressing room rolled past us.

"I have to go." He spun on his heel and stalked off, leaving his cup of coffee behind.

"Hey, if you think Ryker would like to train his Pokémon with me and the guys, tell him to hit me up on Snapchat or Instagram." I ran after him as best I could on skates while carrying a cup of hot coffee. "Or, you know, I could give you my cell number and you could pass it along to him."

He hit a dead stop. A rear-end collision nearly occurred. When he turned around, I held out his cup of coffee and gave him my most disarming smile.

"My son Ryker?"

I snorted. "No, Captain Picard's second-in-command. Of course, your son Ryker."

"Your phone number?"

Was he always this slow? I didn't recall him being so dim. Had he taken a hit to the head that I wasn't aware of?

"Yeah, it's a series of numbers that you dial and it connects you to—"

"I'm familiar with the concept of what a phone number is, Rowe."

Ow. Last names. "Sure, yeah, of course you are. So, uh, you want my number… to give to Ryker?"

He took the coffee with care to ensure our fingers didn't touch in any way. Which was probably for the best, because things had gotten really crackling hot back there for a second. Getting hooked up with Mads would be bad for so many reasons. I couldn't think of one at that moment, but I was sure there were plenty. His blue eyes had darkened just a bit.

"So, what do you say? You want my number or not?"

FOUR

Mads

I took his number. I went to make a note of it on my phone's notepad, but Ten tutted and took it off of me and thumbed one-handed through options. All the time, I couldn't stop looking at his bent head, and when he handed the phone back to me I was disappointed that I couldn't stare without being noticed. His dark hair had this intriguing swirl in it that meant he rocked the style he wore. Me, I kept my blond hair short—nothing fancy for me. I bet Ten spent a long time in the bathroom in the morning.

Don't go there.

"Tell him you have it, right?" Ten said to me.

I nodded, pulling myself back from the very start of an interesting fantasy. Good job, too, as I didn't like the idea of an inappropriate hard-on in a public corridor.

"Okay, then," he said, and left me standing.

I felt like I should be thanking him, or reassuring him that I would pass the information on to Ryker. I did neither. The best thing all around was for me to stay well away from Ten.

And that was mostly how it went. If I saw him heading to the quiet space, I avoided it. If I needed a forward to work with my guys, I chose someone other than Ten, and Ten never called me on it. Why would he? I was a coach; he had to do what I said. Thing was, I couldn't take my eyes off his flicky hair, and the brightness of that stupid tattoo. In fact, everything about how I was reacting to Ten was ill-advised.

It was the morning of checkup day, the bi-monthly poke-and-prod that kept my health insurance intact and the Railers happy.

I'd inherited this shit from my dad, much as I'd inherited his blue eyes, and my blond hair from my mom. When I'd researched Brugada Syndrome I'd seen straight away that I didn't even fit the criteria; Brugada Syndrome is more common in Asian men, but by no means exclusive to them, and I'd had no symptoms before the dramatic collapse out the back of a game. Still, if any late-twenties white guy was going to have this thing in them, it would be me. I didn't do anything by halves, and it seemed even my heart was special.

It had stopped me playing. Dead. Done. But it wasn't enough to stop me living, or coaching.

"How are you feeling?" Doc asked, and I gave him all the usual answers—that I was good, and positive, and hadn't continued to think that maybe losing hockey was reason enough to take my own life.

A year of therapy and knowing I needed to live for my son had put paid to that completely.

"Caught young Ryker on YouTube," the doc said with a grin. He was in his sixties, an expert in heart conditions, and he watched YouTube—go figure. "He has a wicked slap shot."

"He does."

"You must be proud."

"I am."

And I was. So damn proud. With the all-clear and some more chat about hockey, Ryker, and a prescription for meds, I left. As soon as the cold air hit me, I breathed deeply, imagining the ice freezing inside me like it did when I stepped onto a rink.

I wasn't done with this imperfect/perfect life of mine. I wasn't done with any of it.

"COACH MADSEN?" I turned on my skates at the sound of my name, and recognized Deidra from the office. She always looked so small, but then five-two in a room of six foot plus men on skates would make anyone look small. She also appeared nervous whenever we met. Evidently my reputation preceded me, but what that reputation was, I didn't know. "There's someone here."

"Who?"

"Casey Everett," she said, and stared at me.

Casey? What was she doing here?

"Give me five," I told Gagnon, who nodded and waved me away.

Was something wrong with Ryker? I unlaced my skates at top speed, and slipped on running shoes, jogging through the corridor and down to my office. By the time I got there, in my overactive imagination, Ryker had been involved in an accident, and I had even pictured myself driving out of there to get to him.

But it wasn't Casey I saw first. It was Ryker himself. And he didn't look hurt physically, but boy, my son sure looked like a stereotypical teenager—sullen, pissed, his shoulders slumped. And Casey was stone-faced, ashen, her eyes red where she'd clearly been crying. I pulled her in for a quick hug, then closed the door behind me.

"What's wrong?" I began. No one said anything. "Why isn't Ryker at school?"

He was in Shattuck-St. Mary's in Minnesota—prestigious, expensive, and destined for greatness in all things hockey. And why wouldn't he be? His grandfather was the respected Jimmy Everett, left wing and alternate captain for the Red Wings until retirement. And his dad? Well, I was his dad, and until that hit and the resulting news, I'd been a damn good hockey player. Ryker had hockey in his blood.

"Tell him, Ryker," Casey snapped, clearly at the end of her tether.

Ryker looked up at me, defiance in his blue eyes, so much like mine. "Grandpa said…"

Now any sentence that starts with the words "Grandpa said" leads to trouble. Jimmy Everett, or Ev, as he was known to his thousands of adoring fans, liked nothing better than telling his daughter and grandson all kinds of shit. It had started from day one. Literally the morning after the night before, or some mornings later, when she'd told him she was keeping her baby at fifteen. He'd nearly killed me when he'd found out it was me who'd gotten her pregnant. He'd found out because I'd told him. I'd stood next to her, as frightened as any kid could be, and I owned up to what we'd done.

Yeah, I still have the scar from where he punched me. It's faded, but it's right under my chin where I hit the corner of his desk on the way down.

I don't blame him for that. I was stupid, I got carried away, but I was responsible, okay, and I stood by her. I wasn't allowed to go to the house, but I sneaked into the hospital and held Ryker for a few seconds when he was only hours old. Just that tiny touch was enough for me to have him in my dented heart for the rest of my life.

Not that Ev had been happy about that. He'd had me sign everything over, the life of my kid, and I'd gone along with it. Because Casey had looked at me and she'd been crying, like she was now, and I'd just been done. She didn't want me in the baby's life, I wasn't a fit father, I was a kid. So, I'd buried myself in hockey, third round draft to the Sabres, and I'd made money for my child.

Ev, the fucker, had always been there, always knowing best, and even when Casey and I had come to a private arrangement to share custody of Ryker, he'd got high-priced lawyers to check it over. Any small loophole in the arrangement, and I'd known it would be the last I'd see of my little boy.

Yes, it was a fucked-up situation, but Ryker was mine and Casey's.

"Grandpa said I don't have to stay in school if I don't want to, and he's right."

Casey wiped her eyes and looked at me like I could solve this. "Casey, you want to get us Cokes?" I picked up some change from my desk and handed it to her, and she took it with a wobbly smile of thanks. As soon as she was gone, I went into dad mode.

"You're not leaving school."

"I can and I will," Ryker said, and the defiance was so damn clear. "You don't have any kind of schooling."

"And look at me now," I snapped. "You think I wanted to be a coach? What if I'd wanted to do something else?"

Ryker narrowed his eyes. "You're a millionaire, Jared, and you love this job."

He had me there. I really did love this job, as much as you could love a career that wasn't playing hockey when hockey was all you'd ever wanted. And yeah, I had money stashed away. I wasn't one of those players that had flashy anything—after all, I had a kid to support. Right?

"My name is Dad, not Jared, and that is not the point. Your grandpa is not responsible for you, and you will go to school. Education is important."

"I could be a millionaire by the time I'm twenty-two," Ryker began, and I cut him off.

"If you don't get injured, if you make the draft, if you get selected by a decent team. Those are all maybes, but an education is important."

"I'm not sitting here listening to this," Ryker snapped, and he stood up. Suddenly he was all up in my face and not the sullen teenager he appeared. Right there and then was the blood he'd gotten from me, the enforcer, the one who didn't back down from fights. Hell, his fists were clenched at his sides.

"You want to hit me?" I asked. Because he freaking well looked like he did. "You can hit me all you want, but you will respect me, you will not make your mom cry, and you *will* finish at SSM."

He stared at me with fire in his eyes, and I watched and waited him out. Something I'd said in that sentence had softened his anger, and I knew what it had been. It certainly hadn't been the line about respecting me; hell, I'd done very little to earn any respect from him, except being there for a few dad kind of things. It had been the part about his mom. More than me, and certainly more than his interfering grandpa.

"I didn't mean to make her cry," Ryker bit out, his fists relaxing, his eyes bright, "but Grandpa said…" He stopped again.

Okay, I could handle this now. "Compromise here; finish up to draft eligibility at least."

"I could be playing now," Ryker said, a hint of hostility back in his voice.

I wasn't letting this go. "And you'll have matured as a player, put on some muscle, honed skills, the hockey program at SSM is insanely good, and you'll come out a better thinker. Strategies, angles, that kind of thing—you could be a captain one day."

"Grandpa says I have instinct and that I have skills that can't be learned at school." The words appeared measured and uncertain, and sounded just like the kind of shit Ev would come out with.

"Okay." I sat down, a trick I'd learned from Coach Benning. He'd explained that it was all about psychology and lowered confrontation levels, and I agreed. Ryker paused for a moment, then sat down opposite me.

"Another year," Ryker offered.

This was good; we'd reached the negotiation stage.

"No deal. Draft year, and then it's your choice whether you defer and go to college or take the chance early on to get on a team."

Ryker looked right at me. He was a good-looking kid, a future bright star, and for a moment he smiled at me, and there was the old Ryker, the kid who played rough and tumble with me. I'd lost out on so many firsts with him—first step, first skate, first day at school—but I was determined to have some say in his career. I didn't want him losing control, hurting himself young. Selfishly, I wanted him to have the career I had lost. He could have the best parts of me, my eyes, my hair, but thank fuck he didn't have my stupid heart issues.

"Okay," he said finally.

I clapped a hand on his shoulder. "I'm proud of you."

He shrugged like that wasn't important, but I hoped it meant something to him.

I opened the door to let Casey in, but it wasn't just Casey standing outside the room. Tennant *freaking* Rowe was there as well, his mouth wide with a smile when he did this complicated handshake fist-bump thing with Ryker.

When I looked at Ryker, I saw my seventeen-year-old son.

When I looked at myself, I saw a man who was heading for thirty-three and feeling every day of that in hockey-sore muscles.

And when I looked at Ten, I knew his age, and I still had doubts.

I saw him as a man, someone I wanted to kiss; an irrational thought that wouldn't leave me alone. He wasn't gay, or bi, or even curious, otherwise Brady would have said something, or hell, someone would have made a big deal about it.

Look at me lusting after the straight guy.

"I need to get back," I explained, although Ten and Ryker were talking, and it was just Casey who heard. I pulled her in for a hug and whispered the details of my and Ryker's agreement into her ear. She looked grateful.

When I left the three of them outside my office, Casey and Ryker were hugging and Ten was looking right at me. I couldn't make out his expression. I wasn't sure I wanted to know why he was staring at me with that curious half smile. He saw a dad, a coach, and he was friendly with my son.

I couldn't have anything else. I didn't want anything else.

My walls were up, and I wasn't letting them down.

SO, when the shit hit the fan, I wasn't ready for it. We were two days out from our first pre-season game, the team from Jersey was visiting, and the buzz in the room was good. Alongside my defense gelling with the addition of Mac and Arvy in the lineup, the forwards were looking good.

Not that I was looking—or indeed staring—at Ten.

Much.

He was on fire, running circles around his teammates. My only concern as an observer was that he was centering the second line, and his lineys couldn't quite keep up with him. They tried, but Ten had a quick mind, even quicker instincts, and he was passing and they weren't there to receive, leading to too many turnovers. What did we do, though? Get him to slow down, or put him on the first line where he really belonged?

I was sure the speed issue would settle down, but I knew for a fact that Ten's left wing, Lee Addison, a seasoned pro in his seventh year, was getting frustrated. I'd seen it happen over the course of that day's practice session—some shoving, a bit of cursing, but mostly it was harmless. Russian Stan was in net, and we were running three-on-two drills, each line going against one of my pairs. I had an idea of who I was putting with whom, and enough notes to back it all up when we had strategy meetings after practice.

I heard the fight before I saw it, but skated over on instinct, sliding to a halt and attempting to work out what the hell was going on. A quick head-count had five guys beating on each other, and right in the middle, Ten.

Coach skated alongside. "What the fuck?" he shouted, and blew his whistle.

Three of the fighters backed off, but Ten and…shit, that was Addison, his linemate. They were still going at it; Ten sliding back, losing his footing and falling on his ass, dragging Addison with him in a tumble and tangle of arms and legs. The crack of a breaking stick had me wincing, and I waded through the shocked observers to the two on the floor. Ten was on the bottom to start with, but by the time I reached him, he was straddling Addison and shouting in his face.

I couldn't make out the words, not clearly, but I winced at what I did hear. Fag. And that was from Ten. Disgust and disappointment welled inside me. Ten knew me, knew I'd had a boyfriend. He wasn't a kid who crossed lines like that. I gripped his jersey, and with a tug so hard he flailed, I dragged him upward. Temper made me see red, and I yanked him across the ice. He couldn't get purchase, off balance, and almost crashed to the rubber when we stepped off the ice.

"Jesus, Mads," he said, and righted himself with a hand on the boards.

"With me," I snapped.

The forwards coach skated over, but I waved him away. I was dealing with this, and even though he frowned, my counterpart let it go.

"Five minutes," was all he said. "Then he's mine."

I stamped my way to the changing rooms and through to the skate-sharpening area, which was sound-proofed. I had words to say, and I wasn't leaving them unsaid. Ten came in after me, and I shoved him aside so I could shut the door to my office.

"What the fuck?" I asked with restrained aggression.

"He fucking started it!" Ten said, touching the lump on his forehead. "Asshole."

That defense meant nothing to me, and it was my turn to snap. I backed him up against the door.

"If I ever hear you using that word again, I will personally knock you the fuck out."

47

I was shouting right at him, eye to eye, and I saw the moment when the temper in his eyes became something else. Confusion.

"I didn't... I wouldn't..."

"I heard you, Ten. You called him a fag—"

"No," he interrupted me, and he sounded so hurt—defensive, almost. "He called me that, said I was showing him up, that I needed to slow the hell down, and then he called me a faggot, and I lost it, okay?"

Now it was my turn to be confused. "I heard you say..."

"That if he ever used the word fag again, I would bury him."

"Why?"

"Why what?" Ten looked at me like I'd grown a second head, like I had something on my face. He was trying to find something there, and all I could show him was confusion.

"Did you do that for me?" I asked, and abruptly all my strength left me and I slumped against the wall for support.

"Jared—"

"Don't do that, okay? I'm at peace with who I am, but I don't need you to fight for me, you get that? You keep yourself safe and you don't rise to what anyone says."

"That's bullshit," Ten snapped. "That word is offensive and I don't want it used in that way, demeaning, laughing. I won't have it."

"Why? Ten, there are ways of dealing with this. Official ways."

"He kept saying it, and he knew..."

"Knew what? About me? The world and his wife know I'm bi; I don't need protecting." My confusion was growing, and Ten looked like someone had kicked him in the balls and left him to cry in a heap on the floor.

"He saw me, he must have…"

"Ten?"

"Okay, so it's no big deal, right," Ten began. "I took a guy back to my room when I first got here, and he saw."

"What are you saying?"

Ten looked at me. "You're not stupid," he said. "I'm gay, Jared. I'm in the fucking closet, and I'm gay. Okay?"

With that, he left and shut the door behind him, and I was frozen to my chair. I rested my elbows on my desk, then scrubbed my face with my hands.

Abruptly, everything I felt and wanted was right there for me to take.

And I realized I was in shock.

FIVE

Mads
_____

I followed him as soon as it hit me what he'd said. He was gay. He wasn't out. He'd got into a fight with Addison, who knew he was gay?

Did his family know? Why hadn't Brady told me? Surely, I could be trusted to have Ten's back if he needed help on a new team.

The enormity of what Ten had just told me was too much for me to process, and I had so many questions.

"Jared!"

I turned at the voice, part of me hoping it was Ten, part of me dreading it, even though it didn't even sound like him.

Coach Benning stood at the end of the corridor, arms over his chest, and he looked a long way past pissed.

"My office," he said, and pushed open his door, gesturing for me to go first.

"I need to clear something up first," I began, but he frowned and shook his head.

If this was about the fight and me taking Ten off the ice like I had, then I needed to confront and deal right away. Then I could find Ten and talk to him and ask him questions. So many questions.

Resigned, I went into Benning's office, taking in the disorganized mess that was so unlike the repressed, organized kind of man Benning was. And there was Ten, hunched over in one of the guest chairs.

"Ten?" I asked, but I didn't need to ask him what this was about; I knew what was happening here. This was no rebuke to me; this was way more serious shit than that.

Coach shut the door and moved behind his desk, sitting and lacing his hands on the surface.

"Ten has just made an announcement," Coach said, and there was anger in his voice, alongside resignation. "As the team's specialist in equality, this is something you need to hear."

Specialist in equality? That wasn't in my contract. Since when did I have that label? What Coach really meant was that as the only one in the building who had openly admitted he liked cock, I was some kind of expert.

"Ten?" I asked again.

"I'm gay," he said simply. Calm as you like, his gaze not wavering from being focused right on Coach. He wouldn't even look at me.

"Okay," I said, just as calm, like this was the first time I'd heard the news and I was coming from a stance of inclusion and fairness to all players.

"And the reason I fought Addison is that he knows and used words that offended me."

Seemed to me that Ten had been practicing those words, but only someone who knew him like I knew him, or at least thought I knew him, would have been able to hear the anxiety in his tone.

It was the same clipped tone he'd used whenever his brothers had pushed him too far when they were kids. Like he was *this* close to snapping and had to try really hard to keep himself steady and in control.

Coach stood. "You need to fight fires," he said to me. "You have the room, and I'll send Addison in. Management will need to know."

I stood as well. What was Coach saying? He was leaving his office, and… what? I was the one who was going to be handling this shit, when all I wanted to do was get very personal with Ten and ask him how the hell he'd managed to keep this secret for so long.

"Coach, this isn't my remit," I began, and caught Ten glancing at me with hurt on his face.

I wasn't backing down, though. As a friend, I would be there for Ten, but as an employee of the Railers I wasn't the expert in equality just because of the sex I had. Right?

Coach stopped at the door, one hand on the handle. "I'll discuss a salary enhancement with management commensurate with your new responsibility." And with that he left.

All I could think was that I didn't need money. I didn't want to be the team's equality spokesman. And hell, I didn't want to be there with Ten at that moment. I turned from the door and leaned on it; at least that way we'd have some warning of Addison coming in.

"Your family?" I asked in shorthand, knowing Addison would be there any minute.

Ten didn't turn to face me. "They don't know."

"How the hell… Jesus, Ten… Your family…"

Ten stiffened in his seat but still didn't turn, and he didn't say anything else.

There was a knock on the door, and I moved away to open it. A contrite Addison, with a butterfly bandage on his forehead and blood on his jersey, stepped in.

"Coach sent me," he said, and he slipped into the other visitor chair that I had just been sitting in.

Which left me in the Coach's chair, like a principal handing down punishments for school violations. I could, at least, see Ten from this angle, and he looked like nothing I'd seen before. Deadly serious, frozen, unmoving. Next to him, Addison was a mess, his eyes bright like he wanted to cry.

I can't deal with this shit.

I needed some kind of handbook on sensitivity training, I should be sitting there with all the right words, knowing exactly what to say. Maybe I could contact You Can Play, or better yet, they might have something on their website. Why didn't the team already have someone in place?

What if I needed someone to talk to myself, as a bi man? Who was going to help me if I needed it?

I cleared my throat, and Addison jumped like I'd cocked a gun and pointed it at him.

"Who wants to go first?"

Ten said nothing, and Addison kept fidgeting.

I picked up the nearest object to me, one of Coach's fancy pens, and methodically pulled the whole thing into its constituent parts, waiting for one of them to say something.

"Fuck," Addison began, the first to break. "I'm sorry, Ten, I really am."

"Uh-huh," Ten said helpfully.

"It's just, I'm not first line, okay? I can't do this with you. You're too fast, and my contract is up for renewal, and… fuck, I just lost it."

Addison sounded miserable, and I looked at Ten to gauge his expression. There was a twitch of reaction, a tension in him, and I saw him briefly close his eyes. I considered stepping in at that point, wrapping up the meeting now that the apology had been offered, but Addison hadn't finished.

"And my cousin is gay, you know, and I would kill anyone who said that to her with all that hate. You have to know it was heat of the moment, and if I could take it back, I would."

Ten nodded, then turned to face Addison. "Is that the first-cousin you fucked and had kids with?" he asked, clear as day.

I didn't have time to react, Addison got there first. "What the fuck?" he snapped, shocked.

"That's what you hicks do in your state, right?"

Addison opened and shut his mouth like a goldfish, and then something snapped between them and Addison offered his fist, which Ten bumped, and I realized what Ten had done. He'd insulted Addison with the worst cliché he could think of, and Addison had seen it for what it was.

"Now we're equal, right?" Ten said. "No need to walk around avoiding me—we have a game to win."

"I'm so sorry, man," Addison said again.

"Sorry I split your forehead open," Ten offered, "and for implying you fuck your cousin."

"Fuck, it was a good one," Addison said, and touched the wound on his head. "Did you see the blood? It was, like, all over the ice."

They both smiled, bumped fists again, then turned expectantly to me.

Great, now it was my turn.

"We are an inclusive organization, and welcome all orientations," I began, and saw the smirk beginning on Ten's face. I hated him so much at that point.

"Fag is a bad word," Ten said, simple and to the point.

"As are faggot, bum bandit, shirt lifter, and any and all variations on those."

Addison nodded. "Agreed. I won't use them again."

"Although," Ten said, "turd burglar was a new one on me."

"Thanks," Addison said. "I will ensure from now on that I don't use homophobic language, and I also won't tell anyone else on the team what I know unless you decide to make it public."

He stood up, as did Ten, and they semi-hugged, with plenty of back-patting. I honestly couldn't believe what I was seeing.

"Nice talk, Coach Madsen," Addison said, and let himself out.

"Neither of you were taking that seriously," I said as soon as the door shut.

Ten simply looked at me, and his expression was deadly serious. "That there was exactly how it needed to be handled—a one-on-one apology. I won't make this bigger than it is. This is me, my identity, and I won't sit here and let you tick boxes to define me and who I am, or how people talk to me."

"Fag—"

"Is wrong. I know it, you know it, and one day it won't be used again. One day I won't want to kill someone in a face-off because he casually throws it around in every sentence, like punctuation."

"Ten—"

"I have to get back."

I let him go, because I didn't know what I wanted to say at that point. I sat there for the longest time. Was Ten right? Was the way toward inclusion for the guys to be accepting among themselves? Would that spill outward to coaches and management and to fans of hockey? Being bi somehow gave me a pass. I slept with women as well, so people considered me undecided, which was complete crap, but I didn't push it.

No one judged me, and anything that was ever said to me, I ignored. Maybe I should have dropped gloves over slurs. Maybe I should have been the one to start the revolution.

By the time I got outside, Ten was long gone, and he didn't reply to my text asking to meet up.

And I resolved there and then that I needed to get the inclusivity, sensitivity, equality training, or whatever it was called, and really try to do some good.

SIX

Tennant

My first preseason game in the Railers colors, and my head was off in the cosmos. Totally pulling a *Doctor Who*, my brain was skipping through time and space, then landing in some foreign place where I'd step out of the blue box that was my head, look around at the alien red landscape through my 3-D glasses and say—in a spanking British accent—"Nope. Not a clue where the hell I am!" Then I'd go back into the TARDIS and try another planet, where the same scenario would take place

"Hey, Rowe, we doing any training after the game?" I shook off the time travel stuff and looked at one of my teammates. He was shaking a new pack of Pokémon cards in my face. "I'm close to getting my Squirtle to his second evolution."

"Yeah, good. Hit me up after the game and maybe we can set something up."

I got a grin and a slap on the back.

I looked over at Stan seated beside me. His gray eyes roamed over my face. "Plop, plop, fizz, fizz?" the gigantic Russian asked.

"Do you live in TV Land or something?" I enquired. Stan quirked a thick, dark eyebrow. "No, dude, I'm not sick, just spaced out."

"Ah! Space. Final frontier."

"Totally."

He grinned because he thought he had figured it out… I guess. I wasn't sure how much of what anyone said to Stan he understood, aside from the translator who helped him with media stuff. He seemed happy enough, though. Wished I could get to that happy place. Coming out to Mads had been epic and terrifying all at once. I mean, on one hand it might be okay to have a man to talk to about gay stuff… not that he was gay, he was bi, but seriously, he got it. Try sitting in a room filled with guys talking about pussy all the time when you're gay. It's like being a vegetarian in a room filled with meat-eaters discussing all the steak and pork they've had or plan to ingest.

Management knowing was another story. Soon the whole team would know, or maybe already did. Did management want me to come out publicly? My family didn't even know yet. I'd have to tell them first. Christ, I did *not* want to have to do this. I just wanted to play hockey and see Mads smile at me in the morning as we shared the same pillow. Simple pleasures, you know?

Stan stood up, plunked his mask onto his head, and walked out of the dressing room. I looked at the clock over the door.

"Fuck."

I rushed to finish dressing and taping. Maybe being on the ice would center me. It always had before.

There was no avoiding Mads or his blue eyes, but I did my best. And he didn't push in any way. I did catch him looking at me with concern once from the other end of the bench, but the game took precedence. The sound of my skates cutting ice began to gather my thoughts and weave them back together. We were playing New Jersey tonight. And yes, I knew it was a nothing game. All preseason games are. They're mostly to get the lines figured out and gelling while helping the coaches whittle down their rosters. So, while the games counted for nothing standings-wise, there was pressure. I felt it even though I was pretty sure I'd have a starting spot. See, I was out there to get the first line center position. I'd play second line if that was where I was assigned, but I wanted first line bad. And our captain, he felt me breathing down his neck. He knew the young guy was hot for his spot. Whether that spurred him to play better or not, only time would tell. I knew that I was going to play balls to the wall.

The first twenty minutes had been damn sloppy, but it always was. I'd never played with any of these men, and so timing was off. Some hadn't come into camp in great shape, although most had. Those who were slow were dragging down those of us who had worked all summer to stay in shape and hone our skills.

The second period broke open a little about the same time the goalies were switched, which was ten minutes in. New Jersey coughed up the puck at the red line, the cross-ice pass from one winger to the other easily picked off by a center with legs. That would be me. I passed it along to one of the defensemen, since we were heading for a line change. He banked it off the boards for some unknown reason, and New Jersey gobbled it up. Our backup goalie was cold from sitting, and the weak slap shot rolled right through his five hole. I sat down on the bench and listened to Mads shouting at his defensive players. When it was time for us to be on the ice, I climbed over the boards filled with determination.

My chance came quickly. The puck had been dumped

into the visitors' end. One D-man for Jersey was behind the net trying to tangle up Lee, while the other defenseman in red was off puck-watching, even though he knew he should have been in front of his goal. Being the good kind of guy that I am, I filled his slot in the goal. And what do you know, the puck found its way to my stick, and with a flick to elevate it over the goalie's shoulder, it was in the Jersey net. Boom. Pretty as you please. Red light flashing, hugs from the team—including Lee Addison—and lots of knuckle-bumps. God, I loved this sport. It was the only steady and constant thing in my life right now. Once I was seated and a different line rolled out, I removed my helmet and toweled off my head. Peeking down the bench through the damp cotton, my gaze touched Mads, and the swirling space-and-stars stuff started again.

Huh. Maybe it wasn't hockey at all that was turning me inside out. Maybe it was Mads. He inclined his head. I did the same. My gut flipped over. Right. Yep. Cool. There it was, then. I was officially crushing on my coach, who just happened to be older than me, and was also my brother's friend. *Way to rock the good life choices, Ten.*

We managed to win that first preseason game, but just. The coaches had some work to do slimming down the roster, and we players had some work to do bulking up our performances. It would come, though. But me, for now, I was going. I needed to get some space from the dressing room, the guys, the smell of sweat and hockey gear, and the sight of Jared Madsen passing by every ten minutes. He never once said anything or did anything that would be considered... well, considered even friendly. Guess you'd call his behavior aloof.

I slid behind the wheel of my Wrangler. It was only four in the afternoon, the matinee game ending with plenty of time to whittle away. Traffic was non-existent leaving the barn. I slipped some Marianas Trench into the stereo, the music making my fingers tap as I waited at a red light a block from the arena. I threw a fast look to the left, and my mouth fell open. There in the big window of a second-hand shop sat an upright piano.

"No shit," I murmured as "Stutter" blared out of my car speakers.

Some asshole behind me hit his horn. I jumped, pulled out of traffic, and slid into a parking spot right in front of the store. I nearly fell on my face getting out of my Jeep. I hustled to the window, my fingers resting on the dusty glass. I felt like a kid staring at puppies. Instead I was a grown man in a suit smiling at an abused upright piano. Damn, she was in rough shape. Her blonde wood was dented, gouged, and covered in fruit stickers. She probably sounded like shit, but still made me feel an instant connection to my mother. I was so twisted up inside... so lost and confused over my feelings for Mads... it was stupid to be missing my mother simply because I'd seen some shabby old piano in a window, right?

I went inside. The shop was stiflingly hot and dusty. An old man emerged from amid the shelves of old coffee pots, colanders, and other household goods. The dude was ancient, short, frowning and bearded.

"How much for that piano?" I asked before he could introduce himself. "Whatever you want for it, I'll take it. Can you deliver it to my place today?"

By the time I left, I'd spent two hundred for the piano and eight hundred for the old man to get his sons to deliver the decrepit thing to my apartment. Yeah, I'd been taken to the cleaners, but two hours later I had the world's ugliest piano in my space. Sure, some would say that having an upright piano when you didn't have an entertainment system was stupid. Those people, obviously, had not been raised by Jean Rowe. Mom had always said that the arts were just as damn important as athletics—maybe even more so, because one could play piano longer than one could push a puck. I sat on the old bench, smiling like some sort of half-baked goof while paging through several of the old books of sheet music the shopkeeper had thrown in for free. I pulled one out of the damp-smelling box and placed it on the music rack. I'd toss them all into the storage area of the bench once I was off it.

I ran my fingers over the keys and was shocked to hear that it was in tune. It had been a couple of years since I'd sat down in front of a piano. Mom would be thrilled. Grinning widely, I dug into my back pocket, pulled out my phone, and dialed my mother. She answered before the third ring ended.

"Mom, hey. Guess what I just bought."

"Tennant, I'm in the middle of a movie with James—"

I tapped out a couple of notes with my index finger.

"Is that a piano I hear?"

"It sure is. Upright. Found it in a thrift shop. Some kid plastered fruit stickers all over the sides, but it sounds tight. Want to see it?" I asked, knowing she would. Within two minutes, I had her on a video call.

"My gosh, Tennant, I remember playing on one like that for years when I first started teaching. Oh! Let me dash to the Steinway and we can play something together like we used to back before hockey took over."

"Okay," I said, and sat back as she whisked her phone up and ran to her music room.

It had once been Dad's den. His man cave had somehow ended up in the basement and Mom's music room had taken over. One whole wall was nothing but glass sliding doors that looked out on our back porch. Each Rowe boy had spent thirty minutes every night getting instruction in our chosen instrument. Guitar for Brady, sax for Jamie, and piano for me. My brothers say I chose piano because I'm a suck-up, since Mom's first love was piano. Sometimes she joked that Dad was second fiddle to her piano.

"I'm so excited." She sat down and got her phone situated on the music rack of her beloved Steinway. "Are you thinking of picking up your voice lessons again?"

"Mom, when would I have time for vocal lessons? I probably won't have time to play this old girl much." I ran my fingers over the gouged wood.

"You have a voice, Tennant, a damn good one. You should train for the day when hockey won't support you anymore."

"Mom, I'm twenty-two. I think I have a few good years left in me. You want to play a song together, or you want to harp about singing lessons?"

She made a sour face. "Fine, we'll play, but I want you to keep vocal lessons in mind."

"Yes, Mother. Pick your tune." I wiggled around on the bench, rolled my head, and stared at my mother getting herself settled. She pulled the pink sweater around her shoulders off. Oh man. Shit was getting serious now. She'd taken off her sweater.

"Do you remember any of the classics?" she asked as she lifted the fall board on her Steinway.

"Concertos and stuff?"

"And stuff? Honestly, Tennant. How about "Für Elise"? You always enjoyed that one." She sat up straight and proper, waiting for me. "Or we could warm up with "Turkish March" if you're feeling cheeky."

"Nah, I'm good with Beethoven. Then I get to pick one."

"Remember your finger techniques."

"Mom, can we just play?"

She gave me a wink and nodded at me to begin. The first few notes were a little rocky. Mom chirped at me to keep my fingers up. I eased into the piece, and then we rolled into that damn march of Mozart's. Well, Mom blew it to bits. I kind of played backup. We'd glance up from the keys from time to time, see each other jamming, and smile at each other. The footwork came easily, but my left hand fumbled along, as it always did on this song.

"Mom. You are wicked skilled," I told her after we had to end the song due to my major botch-job. She waved off the praise. "Okay, why don't we do this one?"

I hit the opening chords to "Goodbye Yellow Brick Road", and Mom bounced like she was at an Elton John concert. She'd been to twenty. No kidding. Twenty concerts. She adored Sir Elton. The man was her keyboard god. Dad teased her about being a Piano Man groupie. All of us knew that if Sir Elton ever knocked on our door, Mom would run off with him, the fact that he was gay of no concern to her at all.

"Sing for me, Tennant."

Like I could not? I sang for her because she'd asked and because I missed her. I so wanted to talk with her about Mads and the feelings that were growing inside me for him. But I couldn't, and it hurt. Mom and I had always talked about everything. Everything but my being gay, that was... I stumbled over the lyrics, winced a little, and got back to focusing on the song. My voice wasn't anything great, despite what she said, but I sure did like playing and singing. When I glanced up, Mom was rocking back and forth on her bench, pretending she was holding a lighter over her head. That broke me up. My fingers slid from the keys as I laughed out loud. It was during the lull in the concert that I heard the knocking on my door.

"Crap, someone's at the door. Be right back."

I jumped up and left Mom at the piano. Smiling at our silliness, I tugged the door open. There stood Mads, looking at me with humor in his incredible blue eyes.

"Hey," I said.

"Hey." His smile made all my language skills evaporate. My eyes skated up and down his body. Jeans, hoodie, smile. Sin on legs.

"Nice hoodie." *Oh. Wow. That was stellar, Tennant, since, you know, he's wearing a Railers hoodie just like the one you have. You are a moronic dick-slipper.* "They look good on anyone." *Did that compliment sound bad?*

"You should have said that with a strong Rodney Dangerfield inflection."

I snorted stupidly and nodded.

"You have no clue who Rodney Dangerfield is, do you?"

"No, I really don't."

"He's a comedian." Mads had that same weary look my parents got when they talked about dial-up internet, eight tracks, and Sassoon jeans.

"I listen to a lot of Bo Burnham." And now it was time for Mads to look blankly at me. "He's a comedian."

"Christ, I'm old." He chuckled lamely at his own not-really-a-joke. "I dropped by to see if you were okay. After that fight and our talk? You seemed disconnected and distant from the team during the game, and—"

"Can we hold onto this discussion for a few minutes? My mom is on the phone and I don't want her to hear us talking about this." I jerked my head in the direction of the piano.

"Oh, sure, it can wait."

He started throwing off a vibe like he was going to

leave. I really wanted him to stay and smile at me a little longer.

"No, it can't. I want to talk about it."

That was a lie. I didn't want to talk about the fight or the slur or how it sucked having to worry about people finding out I liked to sleep with men. I opened my door wider.

"Just later, okay? Like, after I hang up," I added softly.

"Sure, that's fine."

Mads stepped into my place. I hurried to close the door so he couldn't bolt like a stray cat. I plastered on a smile and jogged back to the piano. There on the phone sat Mom, sipping something hot from a mug that had white flowers on the sides.

"You remember this guy, right?" I asked, all casual Friday as I sat back down on the bench.

Mads sat down beside me. My mother's face lit up when she saw him at my side. His arm resting snugly against mine made me sunny too. The bench was really too small for two hockey players, but who needs to have both ass cheeks on their seat?

"Jared, how are you? Brady said you were coaching defense on Tennant's team." Mom lifted her phone, as if bringing it closer to her nose would make Mads bigger. Parents. Sheesh. "You look good."

"It's nice to see you again as well, Mrs. Rowe." Wow, Mads was all proper parental-unit manners. "I feel good, thanks for noticing. You haven't aged a bit."

Mom giggled. "Oh, stop. You always did have a silver tongue. I'm going to go make myself a fresh cup of tea and get back to my Jimmy Garner movie so you two can talk hockey. Jared, it's been too long. Please stop by sometime. Tennant, make sure you practice your scales and arpeggios daily now that you have a piano."

"Music teachers," I murmured to Mads after we'd said our goodbyes. "You want a beer or something?"

"Water would be better for both of us," he said, then pulled his hoodie up over his head.

I sat beside him, hands on my thighs, and gawked as his T-shirt came up with the hoodie. Thank you, static electricity. I got a great peek at his chest as he struggled to tug off the hoodie but not the T-shirt. The man was seriously cut. Hard, firm pecs covered with fine golden hair. Tight abs that needed to be touched. By me. With my tongue.

"Right, water." I shot up and hustled into the kitchen.

When I returned with two tall glasses of ice water, Mads had gotten his clothing back in place and was flipping through one of the sheet music books that had come with my new used piano. The cubes in the glass clinked against the sides. He glanced up at me standing there staring at him. I held out a glass of ice water. He put the book in front of the other one resting on the music rack.

"I didn't have any lemon or flavoring, so it's just plain Harrisburg city water."

"Yum," Mads joked as he took the glass.

I sat back down on his left and sipped at my chemical-rich water. Mads took a sip, made a face, then gently placed the glass on the floor by his feet.

"When I was a kid, we used to go to this lodge up in Chicopee to ski," he said. "Along one of the slopes, someone—years ago—had run a pipe back into the mountain, and fresh spring water ran from that pipe all year round. I'd always stop and drink from it. It was so cold it would make your head hurt like ice cream."

I nodded.

"That was the best water I've ever tasted."

"Maybe when you retire for good you should move

back to Chicopee and have that water every day," I offered, because he was sounding kind of wistful.

"Maybe I will. So, how are you feeling about things?"

Shit. He'd spun that back around to me fast. I glanced at the sheet music book. It was a Disney one. A few quiet seconds turned into several awkwardly quiet moments. Mads shifted around on the bench. The time had come for me to reply, but I didn't know what to say. Lying seemed shitty. Telling *more* lies, that is. But admitting to him that my feelings were all over the place when he was near didn't seem like the way to go.

"Ten, if you don't want to talk about it, that's fine."

"It is?" I stared at the cubes in my water. They had tiny little air bubbles frozen in them. That was sort of how I felt. Like I had things trapped inside.

"It's completely fine. Why don't you play me a song?"

His request brought my head up and my eyes from my cubes. He was smiling again. Why did he do that? Didn't he know he was deadly lethal to any man when he smiled?

"You do play," he said. "I heard you rocking out in here. I'd forgotten that you did, to be honest. Brady plays guitar, right?"

The last person I wanted to talk about was Brady. "Uh, okay." I bent to the side to put my glass of water on the floor. "What song do you want to hear? I'm kind of rusty, which is why I got the scales and arpeggios comment from my mother."

"And I thought only Aristocats did those."

"Okay, now *that* one I get." I chuckled as he reached for the Disney sheet music book.

"And we thought we'd never find anything in common aside from hockey," he joked, and flipped to a random page then plunked the book back into the rack. "Play this one."

I glanced at the title. Wow. It hardly seemed like the kind of song I should be playing with his hip keeping mine warm. Then again, it *had* gotten Simba some face-rubbing. I'd take a face-rub with Mads. Whiskers on whiskers... Oh man...

"Okay." Playing seemed less dangerous than thinking about his whiskers.

"Are there words?" he asked after I played a few notes.

"Yeah, they're just not on the sheet music. You want the words?"

"Do you know them?" He seemed really into this for some reason.

"Dude, I was brought up by Sir Elton John's biggest fan. I could sing this in my sleep."

That made his smile wider. Yep, I was going to melt, and all those stupid fizzy bubbles trapped inside me were going to float free. Instead of liquefying all over the man, I took a breath in through my nose, let it out the same way, and began playing and singing "Can You Feel the Love Tonight" for him. When the last note faded, I shook off the hold that playing had over me and chanced a peek to the side. Mads looked spellbound or something.

"I told you my finger work was a little weak."

He needed to say something, because I was getting majorly self-conscious. Mads blinked... then leaned in to press his lips to mine. It was a chaste kiss, but it nearly knocked me backward off the bench. His lips were soft but firm, like he was determined there would be no tongues. As soon as my brain touched on tongues, he sprang up from the bench as if he'd sat on a hornet. I heard him kick over his glass of water, but that was the last of my concerns.

"That was not supposed to happen," he coughed as he aimed himself at my door.

I climbed over the bench.

"That was not supposed to happen," he repeated.

"Why not?" I asked as I cut him off at the door.

The man was beyond rattled. He was freaked out, blue eyes darting all over the barren room, looking for an escape route.

"*Why not?*" he barked, his hands twitching like he had no clue what to do with them. I wrapped my arms around my middle to protect myself from the gutting that was going to happen. "Do you need me to recite the reasons? How about I'm your damn coach?"

"You're not my coach. You're the defensive coach. I'm a forward."

He stared at me as if I had a mongoose smoking a hookah pipe seated on my head.

"You're nitpicking. The fact is, I'm your coach. It's totally inappropriate." He ran his fingers through his hair, pushing it into weird angles. It made him look freshly fucked and ten times hotter than he normally did.

"Oh, bullshit. It's not like I'm fourteen or something. We're both adults," I fired back.

His jaw worked for a second. "What about Brady?"

"Fuck Brady. Who cares if we get together?"

"I care!" he shouted, then drew himself back from that place he was headed. I hugged myself a little tighter. "Your brother would kill me if he found out I was screwing around with you. And your parents would hate me. They trust me not to force myself on you."

"You wouldn't have to force me. I'd go to your bed willingly."

I bit down on the inside of my mouth. There was no taking that one back. Mads' face fell, all the anger dissipating to be replaced with shock. He looked like he'd been blindsided by Bobby Orr.

"That would be a horrible idea," he said softly, but his eyes... those sky-blue eyes said that he thought it would be anything but horrible. I might not have years of sexual experience, but I knew desire when I saw it in a man's eyes. Mads wanted us to be a thing, just like I did.

"I don't think it would be. From where I'm standing, you and me hooking up would be fucking epic."

The look he gave me opened me up from sternum to navel. *Way to go, Tennant. Next tell him you want to have his baby. Stupid, stupid, stupid.*

"You're too young to understand what the consequences would be. You're not even out."

"Sometimes, Jared, you have to be man enough to say fuck the consequences."

Okay, that was some big talk from a closeted man who was holding his internal organs in by hugging himself like a distressed teenage girl. Watching Jared battle himself was something to see. His nostrils flared, his pupils grew wide, and his breathing hiked up a bit.

Maybe he'd just had enough arguing. Hell, maybe he was as fucked up as I was. Probably so, now that I think about it. Whatever it was that nudged him toward me, I was thrilled for it. Mads took one long step, his chest brushing against mine. He shoved me against the door. I grabbed the back of his thick neck and pulled his mouth to mine. Then there were no more arguments about hockey or brothers or closets. There was just his tongue gliding over mine, his body pressing me to the door, and his hard cock resting snugly against my stiff dick.

Mads rocked against me. I groaned into his mouth, my fingers biting into the nape of his neck. Lust doused my brain. All I could think of was him and me naked, right there against the door, my legs around his waist, his prick sliding in and out of me. That had to happen. His hands slithered down my sides, his fingertips bouncing along my ribs. Up under my shirt his hungry fingers went. I grabbed two handfuls of short, blond hair and pulled. His moan rumbled up from deep in his chest. He liked that. I did it again, this time sucking on his tongue as I jerked on his hair. His hips rotated slowly as he delved deeper into my mouth. His cock, long and stiff, moved across my hip bone. We both inhaled sharply, moist air mingling on our exhalations.

"Jesus Christ," Mads panted, and broke free of my greedy hands. "Jesus Christ," he said again, then shoved me to the side so he could get the door open.

My thoughts were sloppy and slow, lust-addled. I stumbled out into the corridor. Mads stood about five feet from my door, his elbows locked, palms flat to the wall, head between his arms. I think I called his name, or maybe coughed, who knows? His head came up and our gazes locked.

"We cannot do this, Tennant," he stated gruffly before pushing back from the wall and slamming through the fire exit. The man was so eager to leave he couldn't even wait for the fucking elevator.

"Fuck my life," I whimpered as my ass hit the doorframe.

Down I went into a crouch, face buried in my palms. I stayed down there, hiding behind my hands, until my legs grew numb. Then I stood up, using the door jamb to steady my wobbly legs, dragged my fingers under my eyes, and threw myself back into my home and draped myself over my piano. Fuck the water soaking into the carpet. I'd clean it up later, after the ache inside went away. Which meant the water would never get soaked up.

SEVEN

Mads

How I'd made it home, I didn't know. Last thing I remembered was getting out of Ten's building and into my car. And now I was in my kitchen and everything in between was a blur.

The kiss had been hotter than the kinkiest sex I'd ever had. It had been nothing more than the heat of our bodies and the taste of his mouth and, fuck, I'd been close to rutting up against him and coming in my pants like a teenager.

Heat burned my face as I groaned out loud in my empty place and slumped on the kitchen stool, burying my face in my hands. My intentions had been so good; talk to Ten, find out how he wanted me to approach the team. Nowhere in any of my haphazard planning had there been any thoughts of pushing Ten up against the nearest door and kissing the life out of him. I'd probably broken a hundred coach-player rules just by playing to him let alone kissing him. What the hell had I done?

So, Ten was gay—that didn't mean I should launch myself at him just because I could.

My cell phone vibrated on the counter and I ignored it; didn't even look at the name. If it was Ten, then I had no idea what I would say to him. If it was the team, then I was in no fit state to talk hockey when all I really wanted to do was to drive right back to Ten's and fuck him over the nearest surface.

I was still hard, for fuck's sake.

The cell danced again, and this time I looked at the screen, my eyes unfocused until it hit me front and center who was calling.

Brady.

Holy shit, he knows I just went over to Ten's place and practically forced a kiss on his little brother.

I'm dead.

Picking up the phone had been muscle memory, but actually answering the call was somewhere between the dread that he knew and the hope that he didn't.

"Rowesy?" I said, forcing myself to remain calm. As the oldest of the Rowe brothers, he carried the nickname of Rowesy, and falling back into using it was, I think, some kind of defense mechanism—a link back to our days of playing in Elmira.

"Long time no speak, Mads," Brady said. At least he didn't start by calling me a fucker or a bastard. "Mom texted to say you were over at Ten's place."

Shit. He knows. I stood up from the stool; sitting still was for wimps.

"Yeah, y'know," I offered lamely, because who the hell mumbled that kind of shit to anyone? What was I, eleven?

"Yeah, so…" Brady sounded just as uncertain, and this whole non-conversation thing we were having was freaking me the hell out.

I pushed it along. "Yeah?" Because why should I even think of forming an entire sentence at this point?

"How's he doing?" Brady finally asked. His voice sounded echoey, like he was standing in a large room; no doubt one of the massive rooms in his mansion of a place, which I'd only seen on the realtor's site as he was purchasing it. Sue me, but I kept tabs on Brady—after all, he was a friend. Or at least he had been a friend before my *accident.*

"Good," I said.

What else did he want from me? Maybe a play-by-play of the shots Ten had made in practice, or an analysis of his game chances? Maybe Brady just wanted to make sure he was eating right.

Brady sighed noisily. "Can I be honest with you?" he asked, and there was resignation in his tone, like I was the last person he really wanted to talk to. Shame the friendship we'd enjoyed had vanished because I was an idiot with my head stuck up my ass.

It wasn't his fault we'd been playing against his team when I was taken out. Not his fault his enforcer had decided to leave his skates and hit me right in the numbers. Hell, my team had won the Stanley Cup, wiping the floor with Brady's in the next deciding game. Of course, I hadn't been on the ice—I'd watched the whole fucking thing from a hospital bed—but still, there had been purpose in me sustaining my injury; the Cup was everything to a pro hockey player.

If only I'd been able to keep playing.

"Yeah," I said, because Brady was waiting for a confirmation.

"Coach Benning."

"What about him?"

"You keep him off Ten's back, right?"

What? Keep him off Ten's back? Coach? I was confused, and

I must have let out a questioning noise, because Brady kept talking.

"I kept saying Ten should be talking to one of the other teams. He's easily one of the best forwards out there; he'll be a captain one day…" Brady stopped, and I analyzed what he'd said so far. I knew Ten was good. I knew he had a presence about him that made other players stop and watch.

"I know," I said.

"The Rangers wanted him. Hell, the Wings wanted him as well. Real original six teams."

I'd read all the reports, and the rumors were that a lot of different teams had opened talks with Ten's old team with a view to getting Tennant Rowe on their lines.

"He's fitting in well with the Railers," I began, and stopped when Brady huffed. It was at that moment that I went from feeling defensive, as if Brady were going to call me on kissing his brother, and to protective of Ten's decisions.

"You really think the Railers have any chance at the Cup?" Brady scoffed. Yeah, really scoffed, like there was no way a team only in its second year had any chance.

I didn't point out the stats that were on the tip of my tongue; none of them from the year before meant anything now we had Ten centering one of our lines. If we could get him working at the core of the team, we'd have more than a good chance of getting to the playoffs. That was the *idea* of trading what we had for an eighty-plus point maker.

"With Ten we have every chance," I said, firm and to the point. I didn't allow any doubt to trickle into my voice, or to give Brady any room to add yet more shit to this conversation.

Like, he *was* aware I was the D-coach for the team, right?

Brady wasn't finished. "I get that he works hard, I know that, but he needs a team with depth, a good D-strategy... hell he needs a team with history. It will be years before the Railers get to a point where they have any chance of winning. You really want Ten on a team like that? Don't you want to see him raise the Cup?"

I pulled the cell away from my ear and stared at the screen for a moment, and then, friend or no friend, I knew what I was going to say. Maybe it wasn't the best way to act with the protective older brother of the man I'd just kissed against a door, but I lifted the cell back to my ear and said three words.

"Fuck you, Rowesy."

Then I ended the call.

Brady was a good guy—*had* been a good guy—but who the hell did he think he was, calling me and dismissing my work, my team, my fucking career, just to commiserate about his brother being part of the Railers?

Asshole.

ANGER KEPT me going right up until the next morning. I'd run through the whole spectrum of emotion—anger had become regret, which had morphed into disappointment, and I'd ended up right back at the shame of what I'd done.

In some skewed way, what Brady had said yesterday had become less of a statement about the Railers, and instead I'd begun to take it personally. Almost as if he'd actually called me because he knew the thoughts I'd been having about Ten.

When I arrived at the practice rink, I hid in my office. No point in being out where Ten could see me until practice began. Of course, I hadn't entirely thought that through, and when someone knocked on the door, I had a horrible sinking feeling that it would be him.

When I opened the door, deciding I wanted to face this head-on and standing up, not sitting behind my worn desk, it wasn't Ten on the other side of the door.

"Jared." My kind-of-ex-father-in-law stepped in, and I immediately moved back. We didn't see eye to eye, particularly when we talked, and it was only ever about Ryker.

"Ev," I said.

I refused to give him the honorific of Sir, or call him Mr. anything—not after the way he'd attempted to shut me out of my son's life. My contract with the Sabres had paid me millions, which meant I'd been able to hire the best lawyers, but Ryker had been nearly six before I'd got proper access.

"Spoke to Ryker," he said, straight to the point as usual.

I didn't even give him the courtesy of a reply, because I knew this was going to go to shit really quickly.

"You're making him stay at school."

I leaned back on my desk, feeling my coffee mug shift a little where my ass was perched, then crossed my arms over my chest. If Ev wanted to be intimidating, all superior and up in my face, then I was damn well going to show him that none of his shit scared me.

I wasn't that fifteen-year-old kid standing in front of him and promising to look after his daughter anymore. I was twice that age and a couple of years, and only half as stupid as I'd been then. Casey and I were never going to be forever—one split condom and we'd made a life, but that didn't mean we'd ever make it for real as a family. She was married now, to a stockbroker, with three little kids, stepsisters to Ryker, and she was happy.

His lips thinned when I said nothing, and he had that stern, I'm-really-pissed-with-you expression on his face. I did the one thing I knew would annoy him even more; I merely quirked an eyebrow in question.

"He doesn't need an education to be the best hockey player," Ev said. "Why make him do something he doesn't want to?"

I shook my head. "Don't you know, Ev? Pushing our kids to do things they don't want to do is actually in our job description as parents. Like, you know, when you pushed your daughter to block me from seeing my son."

Ev did that whole lip-pursing thing again, and I took a moment to focus on the gray at his temples and the scar on his cheekbone.

"Is there anything else?" I asked, and deliberately looked at my watch in a dismissive gesture. When I looked back up at him, his expression was tight and I could have sworn he was about to explode.

"Mads?" Coach called from behind Ev. "Vid room in five."

He didn't stay to talk. No one stayed when Ev was in the house. Like they knew they'd be walking into a powder keg. Didn't matter that he was one of the old guard who'd seen some pretty cool things; he was known as an asshole among players and coaches, even though no one ever said the words explicitly in front of me.

I guess they thought I felt something for the bastard, but all he was to me was my kid's grandfather. That was all.

I gestured to the door. "If you don't mind, I have work."

I stepped forward, and he stood his ground before turning smartly on his heel and leaving without a goodbye. It was okay, though—I wasn't expecting a goodbye, not when I hadn't even got a hello. To him I was, and always would be, the waste of space who'd slept with his daughter and ruined her life. I agreed with him to a certain extent. If Ryker was out there getting girls pregnant, I'd be pissed.

But one thing I wouldn't do, ever, was keep my grand-children away from one of their parents.

I COLLECTED my stuff and locked my office door, rolling my shoulders to release the inevitable stress that came with every meeting I had with Ev. My cell indicated a text, and I checked the screen. A message from Ryker. *Heads up, GP is visiting.* Ryker called Ev "GP", short for Grandpa. I sent off a quick thanks and added a kiss.

I loved Ryker, and never a day went past when I didn't want to tell him that.

Finally, I was at the door to the video room. In there would be the entire team, including Ten. Part of me thought maybe I should have talked more with Ten instead of doing the door-kissing thing, but it was too late now.

I pushed inside and cast a quick look around the room. Just like with every other team I'd played on right from junior hockey, the lines sat together: the Ds in a huddle, the goalies off to one side looking suitably weird and their gazes as focused as mine. Goalies always wanted to know everything, and had this uncanny knack of seeing way too much.

I moved straight to the front, noting that Ten was two rows back, centering his line, and looked like sex on a stick. He was in the same practice jersey as the rest, the same pads, the same everything, but he was different. He was everything I wanted in one parcel, and he was sitting and waiting for me to make this work.

"Okay, everyone," I began. "Hush up."

One by one, they stopped talking, and interested faces turned my way, Benning took a seat at the back and nodded encouragingly. I met Addison's gaze, and he nodded as well—this was as much on him as it was on me. I shuffled the papers on the small lectern and began to read what I'd taken from the web.

"The NHL is teaming up with the various established projects to create more visibility for LGBTQ inclusion in the league. As part of this, there is a list of team ambassadors, and for the Railers that ambassador is Lee Addison, backed up and supported by myself. Lee has some words for you."

Lee stood up and waved a hand, and was treated to an almost polite set of muted cheers. Looked like the room was full of serious hockey players thinking serious things, some of them a little confused, others who knew exactly what Lee was going to say.

He was very direct in what he said. "You all know what happened. I lost my temper and used a gay slur on a teammate." A couple of players exchanged glances. "I used a word that was filled with every ounce of temper and hate I held inside. I apologized for what I did, and have volunteered to become our team ambassador for inclusion on the team." He sat down, but immediately stood up again. "So, if you need support or help—because let's face it, the shit we say sometimes means gay players stay in the closet, because we are the opposite of inclusive—then you know where I am. And it isn't just the gay thing." He cleared his throat again. "It's race and culture and things like that. I have the support of You Can Play, and also Coach Madsen." He kind of collapsed in his chair, clearly as happy with public speaking as I was.

There was some quiet chatter, then everyone turned to focus on me.

"Let's think about what we say," I said in summary. "Leave the hate at home."

The players left the room in ones and twos, some talking, some quiet, and finally it was me, Addison, a quiet Ten, and Coach Benning in the room.

"We're done here?" Coach asked.

"Done," Addison confirmed.

I wanted to be in the room alone with Ten, so we could talk. I didn't want to be in the room alone with Ten, because I didn't know what to say.

In the end, it didn't matter—Ten left first, with Addison right behind him.

"Anything you want to tell me?" Coach asked.

"I asked for a management meeting at five. Rowe is attending with me."

"Good. Good. Did you talk to Rowe about what he told me?"

"Not as much as I wanted to."

No, I kissed him instead.

"I trust you to deal with this in a manner that won't leave our asses twisting in the wind." Benning was absolutely dead serious, and I knew what he wanted me to say in return. "This could be a big thing for the league, and needs to be handled right for Rowe and the team."

He didn't want me to lose sight of how Ten's admission would affect the team when they found out, or how management might not be as supportive as I wanted. The Railers were a reasonably new team with one hell of a lot to live up to. This was the very start of what everyone hoped would be a long-lived franchise, but one that had a lot of crosses next to its name.

"I will," I promised.

. . .

I LEFT the practice and showered, pulling on clean sweats and my Railers Hockey T-shirt. I like the dusky blue they'd chosen for the team colors. Add in white and gold, and we rocked the teams in looks. Or so I thought. Of course, most of that came from me watching Ten in the uniform, so I was very likely biased.

The door to the coaches' area opened and quickly shut, and I spun to find Ten in my space.

"Mads," he began.

"You shouldn't be in here," I said. Because, yeah, rules were what I should be thinking about right then. Ten's dark hair was wet, pushed back from his face, his beautiful eyes focused right on me.

"I wanted to ask something before this meeting." He looked concerned, like he thought we wouldn't be able to handle what we needed to.

I swallowed as he wet his lips with his tongue. A nervous gesture, and just that small action had me getting hard. Jesus.

"What?"

"Did you... I don't think you did, not really, but..."

"Spit it out, Ten."

"Brady left this message saying he'd talked to you and you hung up on him. Did you tell him about me?" There was pain in Ten's eyes. He looked both confused and concerned, and I knew he was expecting the worst. Carrying this secret was likely eating him away inside.

I reached out and touched a hand to his arm—briefly, because someone could walk in at any time. "I wouldn't do that," I reassured him.

Ten relaxed. "I need to tell them, soon, if I want to..." He looked at me again, then with a sigh he looked left and right before he pressed a kiss to my lips. "I'll see you up there," he said, and left.

And I stood and watched him walk away with so much confusion in my thoughts. I did the whole cliché thing of pressing my fingers to my lips, like I could touch the kiss that had been left there. My chest was tight, and I felt like that single kiss meant much more than I imagined.

Was this more than lust? Was I getting in way too deep with a man a decade younger than me, and a family connection complicated by friendship?

Hell, whatever it was, it scared the living shit out of me.

EIGHT

Tennant

M anagement meeting. Fancy name for facing the GM and others in upper management and telling them you're gay. As I stared at the door that separated me from the owner, GM, and who knew who else, the urge to throw up grew. Then someone touched the back of my hand. My gaze flew to the right.

Mads smiled at me. "I'll be right at your side."

Every atom in my body hummed. I wanted nothing more than to take his hand and hold it throughout this meeting. But we couldn't do that, because rules...

"Thanks." I caught sight of Connor jogging up to us.

"He's the player union rep," Mads quickly explained. "Connor, thanks for joining us. You know why we're here?" he asked as he and Hurleigh shook hands.

"I have a pretty good idea." Connor extended his hand. I slapped my palm over his. He didn't elaborate.

"Thanks."

I'd figured my secret wasn't much of a secret anymore, but hearing that Connor had any idea of what it was made me even edgier. Were all the guys talking about the queer on the team? Judging me differently because we all know gay men are effeminate and couldn't play hockey? Ugh. My gut was a full-blown mess now.

Mads patted me on the back. It wasn't what I wanted —or needed—from him, but for now it was the most he could give me. I threw back my shoulders and knocked. Might as well get it over with. My suit felt hot, the dress shirt scratchy, my tie tight. Some guy in a suit that cost way more than mine opened the door. I walked into the board room. It was filled with older white men in suits. The walls were covered with dark wood paneling. The rich carpeting soaked up our footsteps. A vase of flowers sat in the middle of an oval cherry wood table. Fingers touched my lower back. I knew it was Mads without even looking. His touch did things to me…

The dude working the door closed it and sat back down. I spotted the owner seated way at the other end of the table. He was sipping ice water and staring at me. I cleared my throat.

"I'm Tennant Rowe." *I'm sure they know who you are, doofus.* "And I'm gay." *Bet they knew that too. Yep. No one is surprised. You can go toss cookies now.*

"Kudos for skipping all the rambling pretense and going right for the meat of the matter," Mads whispered.

Connor stepped up and started talking for me. I glanced at Mads and saw all kinds of emotions in those stunning, sexy eyes of his.

Lots of talk took place, most of it incredibly PC and in support of me and any other LGBTQ players who might be on the team. I shook hands with every guy at the table. We talked hockey. Then Mads, Connor, and I were escorted to the door.

"They took that well," Connor said as we walked to the closest elevator. The upper levels of the barn were always hopping with staff and management. "Of course, they really don't have any choice. It's not like they can tell you to hit the road. You have a contract. I don't think being gay violates any morals clause. If you need to contact me for any reason, though, you know where to find me. I'll be on the ice trying to keep a step ahead of you."

"Yeah," I muttered, feeling kind of ashamed of how I was dogging the man. We shook, then Connor left me and Mads by a window that looked out at the parking lot surrounding the arena.

"Don't feel badly for wanting to get his spot, Ten. That's sports. He knew you'd be hounding him."

"He's an okay guy, though," I argued weakly. My stomach was still gross.

"Yes, he is. And you've got the talent he wishes he had." Mads rested a shoulder against the window frame. He looked tight in a dark blue suit that made the flecks of darker blue in his eyes pop.

I glanced up and down the lushly decorated hallway. "What about us?"

"Us is a nuclear detonation, Tennant."

Ouch. "And you don't want that kind of fallout in your life, right? You want to be all safe and sound hiding under your little metal desk."

"Look, don't think you know me so damn well after one kiss," he ground out. "Do you have any idea what seeing you could do to my career?"

"No."

"Neither do I, but I have to think it's *not* going to be a promotion."

I exhaled, then swallowed, hoping the churning acid in my stomach would cease and desist. Throwing up was not on the list of things I wanted to do in front of Mads. The parking lot was damn fascinating.

"Okay, I get it. I'll step back." God, that hurt way more than it should have considering that all we'd shared was one kiss. One incendiary kiss…

"I didn't say I wanted that either." My gaze flew from blacktop to Jared Madsen. "Christ, when you look at me like that, I want to…" He looked up at the ceiling and then back at me, "Well, I want to do things that we probably shouldn't do in a hallway outside the owners' suite."

"Okay, right. I get it. So, uh, where are we? In terms of us?" Excitement bubbled up in my chest. Adding that sensation to the bubbling reflux was nice. Not.

"We're going to see where we go." He smiled gently at me. "And we are going to take this slow, Tennant."

"Cool, good. I can do slow."

He looked like he didn't believe me.

SLOW SUCKED. Seriously, it was the worst. Obviously my slow and Mads' slow were worlds apart. His slow consisted of nothing but touching here and there, long looks, and secret smiles. My slow would have had us at least into some slippery-hot, ball-slapping sex. I spent more time jacking off in the shower now than before he'd said we were going to see where we went. If we didn't get some physical shit going soon, I'd be in the padded room at the nearest mental hospital.

Maybe not getting laid—or even kissed—was good for my game, though. Back in the day, the old coaches had thought so. I *was* playing like a fucking demon, crushing anyone in my path, and sadly that included Connor, the good guy. Nothing personal, but he stood between me and that first line center position. I'd blasted his doors off during the preseason and now, with the last preseason game against Carolina under our belts, all that remained was for Benning to make his final cuts and decide on the starting line-up. If that SOB didn't put me on the first line, I'd—

"More balls."

Stan's deep voice jerked me harshly from my angry daydreams. There were ten of us gathered in my hotel room. A late season tropical depression had blown into North Carolina. Traveling had been called off until the swirling storm moved on overnight, so here the Railers sat, playing Pokémon Evolutions and dreaming about getting on the line they wanted or getting laid. I downed another can of Mountain Dew Code Red. It was my fourth. I felt like I could scale the walls like Spider-Man.

"Ten, you into this?" Addison inquired. He'd joined the training group last week and was kicking all sorts of ass. "You seem spacey."

I tossed my training cards onto the table and stood up. "Too much Dew. I'm wired."

The guys chuckled and play continued without me.

I paced the room like a puma in a cage. "I'm going to see if I can walk this off. Stan, you take my balls."

"Groovy, man!" the big Russian said, then swept my cards from the table.

The laughter faded as I closed the door behind me. Starting that group had been a good idea. I'd grown much closer to several of the guys since we'd started playing. Pity we couldn't lure any of the older players in.

I started off walking the hallway. That didn't burn off the soda fast enough, so I jogged up and down the hotel corridor. When I'd done four laps, I was slightly winded but still cranked. I did what any man who was hard up and running on four cans of red Dew would do. I rode up to the fourth floor, where the coaches were rooming, and pounded on the door of the hottest defensive coach in the eastern division.

Mads opened the door in nothing but dress slacks and an unbuttoned dress shirt. I'd at least changed into some jeans and my favorite *Doctor Who* "Bowties are Cool!" T-shirt after we'd gotten back to the hotel. Not that I was complaining, because he fucking rocked his half-dressed look.

"Hey, Tennant, what's up?"

He looked shocked and more than a little guarded. Did I send off perv vibes or something? Was I drooling? Shit, he looked so good...

"I wanted to talk to you about... uh, about how the defense is playing in the neutral zone and its impact on the forwards." There, that sounded official in case anyone might be eavesdropping.

He eyed me warily like I was something dangerous that had come rapping on his door. A lust demon or a succubus. Could dudes be succubi?

"Come in," he said, then stepped back to allow me to enter.

His room looked just like mine. Basic hotel tan, blue, and white. It smelled of him. His cologne and his unique scent.

"I was just diagramming some plays for the defense. I'd be happy to have your input on them, since there seems to be a problem with—"

I pounced on him. Hungry and desperate, I lunged at him, clapping my hands to the sides of his head. A sound of surprise escaped him before I covered his mouth with mine. I felt him stiffen, like he was going to push me away. Nope. We were not doing that shit now. I lapped at the seam of his mouth, then at the corners. He opened for me and I dove in, starving now for the taste of him. His mouth was wet and hot and tasted of coffee. Mads grunted. The sound amped up my desire even more. I suckled on his tongue until I got the reaction I wanted. When I did—his arms going around my waist—I released his head and grabbed his ass. Frantic for his touch, I rubbed against him, shoving my erection into his stomach. The man groaned again in reply. I made a move to palm his dick.

"My God, you're like a chipmunk pumped full of Red Bull." Mads chuckled breathlessly, trying to pry my hands from his crotch and ass.

"I know, I'm sorry." My hands moved over him, desperate for all the touching they could get. "It's just… I've been dreaming about this for weeks. You and I…doing this, touching, kissing, getting into your bed. I'm wired and grabby. I need more than just a smile during scrimmages, Mads."

"I understand the need." He held my wrists, then pressed several kisses to my mouth. "I've wanted this too, but we're taking this slow, remember?"

"Why slow? I'm ready now."

Since he had my hands, I simply leaned in to lick at his mouth. He steered me toward the bed, fingers around my wrists, kissing me with warm passion in return. His attitude to this whole sex thing was languid and lazy. It was making me insane.

"Have you ever done this before?" he asked, then shoved me into a seated position on the edge of the bed.

I gave him my dirtiest look, then reached for his belt buckle.

He patiently removed my fingers from his belt. "I'd like a little more to go on than that glare."

"Ugh, yes. I've sucked dick before."

"Have you ever had a man inside you?"

A rumble of want rippled through me. Instead of

going for his dick, because he was suddenly all Mr. Chastity about it, I opened his dress shirt a little wider, baring a wide swath of hairy chest and tight abdomen. My cock throbbed in time with my pulse. I pressed a kiss to his stomach, then one to his chest, my thumbs dangling off his belt. Soft, deep noises rolled out of him each time I placed my lips to his skin.

"Tennant, have you ever had a man inside you before?"

"Once," I replied, licking around the edge of his navel.

He placed a hand on my head, murmuring about my hair swirls or something. I glanced up to find him staring at me. He was completely into what I was doing. Our eyes locked, my tongue darted out to taste his bellybutton.

"Only once? Did you use protection?"

I sat up. "You know I'm tested regularly. You've seen all the players' health reports."

"First off, I know that. I also know you could have had unprotected sex on Monday and been tested Tuesday. So, when was it and did you use protection?"

"Yes. It was way back and Christ, you sound like my old high school health teacher. Can we just skip all of this and get to the part where you slide your cock into me?"

"Not tonight," he replied, shucking his shirt off his shoulders.

Now we were talking. I enjoyed seeing it flutter to the floor. I *loved* seeing his naked chest even more.

I pulled my shirt off and tossed it aside, then wiggled back onto the bed. "So why not tonight?"

"Because I think we need to take this slow."

I collapsed back onto the mattress with a dramatic sigh. "Mads, slow sucks. What, are we going to just pet and grind on each other like we're fourteen or something?"

I heard his belt hit the floor. I closed my eyes, eager to

hear more. The sound of his zipper going down followed. My skin itched. My balls grew heavy. The soft shuffle of his pants slipping down his legs filled the room. Then the bed sagged. The weight of him and the hot warmth of his body pressed tight to my side was all I needed. I rolled my head to face him and opened my eyes. And promptly lost everything that I was to him. There was so much in his gaze. Heat and lust, sure, but other things. A little bit of fear and a whole lot of tenderness.

I had to touch him, but he shook his head when I reached for him. Instead, he placed his hand on my stomach, flat palm to abdomen.

"You're trembling," he murmured.

"I want…"

A million things, but how did I tell him that? How could I articulate that I wanted him in ways I'd never wanted anyone else? That I'd dreamed of him, of this moment, of his mouth on my brow and his cock buried in me. Of his breath on my neck in the night and his smile over eggs in the morning? How? How could I tell him all that?

"I do too," he whispered, then slid his lips over mine.

My fingers dove into his hair while his tongue made a deep, hot sweep of my mouth. I tugged softly, getting that low grunt of approval I'd gotten before after doing that. I arched my back from the bed to push my cock into Mads' hand.

"God, but I want," he growled after leaving my mouth to taste my throat.

"Touch me," I panted, fingers wound in his hair.

Mads stuck to his vow, though, the jerk. Even though I was arching up he refused to touch my cock. He rubbed hard circles over my chest and shoulders, pulling me to my side then throwing a beefy leg over my hip. I nipped at his bottom lip, tipped his head back to suckle on his Adam's apple, and gyrated wantonly against his cock as it strained against his boxers.

"I need to lose these jeans."

"Leave them on a bit longer." He kissed my jaw, my clavicle, then tongued a nipple, all the while rocking his hips against me. "I think watching you come in your pants would be incredibly sexy."

"Oh Christ," I moaned, pumping my ass to keep the friction of his dick against mine going. "You'll jerk me off, right? Please, fuck, Mads, you have to touch me."

"Not tonight. Tonight… is just this." He did lower his hand to my thigh, grabbing the meaty part and tugging my leg strongly to intensify each thrust he made against me. "Next time we can go further." Hearing him say that pushed me close. "I want us to be about more than fucking, Tennant."

Yep. Those were the magic words, it seemed. Not something raunchy like you'd hear in gay porn. Nope. I blew apart because Mads told me he wanted more than sex with me. He held on to my leg tightly as I flailed and whimpered. His lips captured mine, swallowing the sounds of a man lost in orgasm, which was smart on his part. We *were* in a hotel with the head coach sleeping on the other side of the wall.

When the tremors subsided, he lifted his head and released my thigh.

"Shit… that was intense." I huffed, then ground a bit harder into him. "Your turn."

"I don't have to come every time we lie down together," he said between soft kisses placed along my biceps.

"Well, yeah, you do. That's kind of the point," I replied, and got a tutting kind of sound.

Swell. Miss Perkins the health teacher was back with

94

another lecture on something that would have me sleeping on my textbook within seconds.

"Oh, impetuous and randy youth," he teased.

I pushed him onto his back and climbed on top of him, my hip bone right on his cock. He sucked air through his teeth when I bumped his dick accidentally-on-purpose.

"Tennant, you're sort of missing the point here. Making love isn't all about the orgasm."

"So, you *don't* want to come?"

He looked up at me, a smile playing on his lips. "Yes, of course, but it doesn't have to be the main objective every single time."

"So, you *do* want to come?"

His laughter was honest and made me grin. "Yes, Tennant, I would like to come, but seeing you writhing under me when you came was incredibly erotic."

"You liked that, huh?" I wiggled my ass around. "Did you have fantasies about making me come, Mads?"

"Every fucking night." He tugged my mouth back to his. I got all wild and hungry, sucking on his tongue while grinding on him. "I jerked off to those fantasies too."

"No shit," I panted over his lips, my hips driving down into him hard. I felt a shudder go through his big body. "Fuck, that's hot." I bumped my budding erection against his prick.

"Christ, you're almost hard again."

He began working at my pants then. Eager, hard tugs on my jeans until they were down over my ass. I wiggled free of the denim, then leaped back into bed. That was when I saw the head of his dick peeping out of the top of his boxers. My briefs felt tight again.

Mads grabbed my hips and held me in place. Then he began jacking me up and down over him. The contact and rasp of cotton was unbearably delicious, just like his scorching kisses and the way he pumped up when I ground down. If only he'd let me get my mouth on him. He rolled me onto my back without warning, his eyes burning with need as I pushed my leg between his. Mouth sealed over mine, he began humping me hard. The bed thumped into the wall with each powerful thrust. I pawed at his back and arms, trying to get enough air into my lungs. Then he came. His head fell to my shoulder and all his ropey muscles contracted. I felt his prick kicking, then the hot flood of spunk soaking through our underwear. My balls tightened yet again and I lost it one more time.

"Tennant, you're going to kill me," he whispered beside my ear, then took the lobe between his teeth.

That off-the-cuff comment startled me. "Is it your heart?"

Of course, I knew about that condition of his. Everyone in the family—hell, the world of professional hockey—knew about his heart. And here I'd been pushing him to have sex. What if he couldn't have sex?

"Shit, I'm sorry. Should you not be doing this? Are you stroking out on me?!"

"Tennant, no, I'm fine. It was a joke." He nipped playfully at my jaw.

"Fuck, man, don't do that to me ever again." I thought I might faint with relief.

"I won't, I promise. But you really *are* going to do me in."

"You'll die smiling, Mads." Coming back with some humor was good—made me feel less freaked. I hoped he was okay with joking about it. "I was kidding about the dying part." I pushed to my elbows so I could press my mouth to his. "Like, you know I was kidding…"

"I know you were," he murmured between soft, searching kisses.

I fell back onto the bed in relief, Jared nestling into me, his weight incredibly appealing as it settled over me.

And that was how the home frottage sessions began. When we were on the road, there was no more petting. Mads had laid down that law after that one night, and I kind of understood it. We *were* walking a fine line with this relationship… if that was even what it was. Being discovered with our pants literally down would be one major mess for Mads and the team. Knowing he was just a few doors down when we traveled was torture. When we were home, I was at his place, because all I owned was a piano and a PlayStation, which he commented on all the time. I found his worry about my undecorated place funny.

Mads was unlike any lover I'd ever had. He was tender, methodical, patient, and determined to take things S-L-O-W. He was humorous, sharp, smart, and totally devoted to Ryker. The only complaint I had was how leisurely Jared Madsen really moved. I'd thought slow would mean a date or two then getting into the monkey sex. Nope. With Mads, slow meant moving at the speed of a fucking glacier.

"I don't want you to regret being with an old man," he said whenever I begged, pleaded, or demanded he fuck me, or at least let me suck that fat, uncut cock of his. I told him repeatedly over that long, incredible month that there was no way I'd ever feel that way, but he stuck to his guns. And along the way, I learned things about taking my time, pleasing my partner, and not being all about the money shot. Each time we came in each other's arms, I grew a little closer to the man, trusted him a little more, and fell a little deeper.

HE AND I both went through a ridiculous amount of underwear from mid-September to Halloween, but I didn't complain. Well, not too much. Okay, I bitched constantly. Then the first weekend of November arrived, and with it the knowledge that we were going up against Boston and Brady in a Sunday afternoon matinee game.

Brady would arrive sometime late Saturday. We were to meet up at this clubby pub down by the Capitol building and do dinner. Mostly Brady wanted to check up on me and touch base with Mads, I assumed. Whatever. I was too busy trying to make Coach Benning acknowledge how much better suited I was for the first line to worry over Brady trying to dictate my life. Benning, the stupid shit, had this mental block about playing the old vets no matter if he had someone faster, younger, stronger, and hungrier. It drove me—and several sports writers—nuts.

While I was shoving clean clothes into an overnight bag, my phone chirruped. It was my mother ringing. Guilt instantly washed over me. Her calls had gone to my voicemail nine times out of ten over the past six weeks. Not that I didn't want to talk to her. I did. It was just Mads. Really, Mads and hockey were my life now. But still, she was my mom…

"Hey there, Mom," I said with all kinds of cheery goodness.

"Tennant, I've been trying to contact you for days. What good is having a cell phone if you never answer it? Your father was starting to worry that you were in a ditch somewhere."

"Right, it was Dad worrying about me in a ditch." I had to chuckle at her. I tossed a handful of clean underwear into my duffle.

"Don't get sassy. There were two reasons I was calling. One was to ask if you've been playing the piano. Have you?"

I glanced at my dusty piano. "No, not recently." *I've been too busy playing hockey and grinding on Mads, Mom.*

"I was afraid of that. Put the PlayStation controller down occasionally and play that piano. You'll thank me someday."

I rolled my eyes but mumbled something to placate her.

"Secondly, you remember Jennifer Gates?"

I froze with a clean T-shirt in my hands. "Uh, yeah…"

"She just completed her studies and has come back home to start teaching kindergarten over at your elementary school. Isn't that exciting? She's staying with her parents until she can find an apartment. Well, you know how much your dad and I always thought of Jennifer, so I invited her and her folks for Thanksgiving dinner. Tennant? Honey?"

"I… Uh, I'm here, Mom, just thinking."

I dropped the shirt I'd been gripping into my duffel bag. Jennifer Gates. Nice, sweet, perky Jennifer. My beard all through high school. Hell, I'd even fondled her boobs the night of junior prom just to keep the ruse going. When she'd moved off to Colorado to get her education degree, I'd pretended to miss her like a boyfriend would miss a girlfriend. My eyes drifted shut. Mom started talking about old times and how Jennifer had always been so smart and clever. Oh, and those big brown eyes of hers always sparkled.

"… after we eat and spend the evening. Maybe you and her can rekindle?"

I opened my eyes and stared down at the bag I was packing to take over to Mads' place. "Mom, can we do a video chat?"

"Oh, sure. Let me grab my coffee." She dashed off.

I sat down beside my bag. The bag holding the clothes

that I was taking to my gay lover's. Wow. Okay. This was not how I'd planned this. Actually, I'd never planned it at all.

"Okay, I'm back. Dad says hi."

"Tell Dad to stick close, okay?"

I got us into the video chat, my fingers shaking so badly I almost dropped my cell a few times. She accepted the call, and then there they were, heads side by side, smiling at me. Nope. No. I couldn't do this. Not like this. Not over the phone.

"Here's Dad." Mom patted his cheek. "He's very happy about Jennifer coming back home too."

Okay. Yeah. It had to be now… like this. Fuck. Shit.

"Mom, Dad, I'm really happy that Jennifer is back home." Mom gave Dad a knowing wink. "But I'm not going to rekindle anything with her because… well, there is nothing to rekindle."

"Oh, Tennant," Mom said as Dad stood bent over behind her, his dark eyes locked on me. "Of course, there is. You took that girl to every dance. She went to all your games and cheered you on. Everyone knew you two were a couple. Why, you and Jen were chosen "Most Likely To Live Happily-Ever-After" in your yearbook."

"She's available, son." Dad chimed in. "Your mother asked."

"Oh God," I moaned.

"I didn't ask Jennifer," Mom quickly clarified. "I asked her mother. You need to make sure you fill in the important details," she gently scolded the man standing behind her.

"Mom, it has nothing to do with the fact that she's available. I'm not."

They both took a second to digest that announcement.

It kind of shocked me too, but now that I'd said it, it felt right. Mads was the only person I wanted to be with.

"Oh, well, you never mentioned you were seeing a new girl…"

I took a deep breath as I stared right into my mother's eyes. "That's because it's not a girl."

And all the air on planet Earth was sucked into a vortex. Had to have been, because breathing got damn difficult. Mom looked shaky. Dad… Dad was spinning wheels for sure.

"Are you saying that you're gay?" Mom finally asked.

I sucked in a huge breath of air and nodded. Mom sat in our kitchen looking at me as if she didn't know me. Dad walked away. I started to tear up. Fuck. My father had just walked out…

"Tennant, oh honey, why didn't you tell us sooner? I wouldn't have pushed Jennifer on you if I'd… Bruce, come back from the window. Dear Lord, he'll think you walked out."

Oh. *My*. God. He'd just gone to look at the back yard. That was what he always did when he was hit with shit out of the blue. He'd go look at the yard while he processed. Said he found the yard calming.

He was looking at the yard. He didn't walk out. Oh fuck. I started crying.

"Tennant? Son. Oh, Bruce!" Mom started crying.

"Son." That was Dad. I cried even harder, my tears splattering on the front of my phone. "Tennant, don't cry. Please. It was just… unexpected news, that's all."

"I didn't want to tell you guys like this…" I coughed, snuffled, then used the shirt I'd just packed to wipe my face and phone. "But the Jennifer thing. Mom, I don't want her thinking there's anything between us. There never was.

Not like that. I lied to her. I've lied to so many people. Dad, please don't walk out again."

"I won't, son. Don't you worry. Not ever."

That made me cry harder. I'm not sure how long Mom and I sat there weeping and trying to talk. We said all kinds of things, the three of us. Most of it was stupid apologies from both sides. I was sorry for being born gay and they were sorry for not being better gay parents, which made me snort-laugh so hard my sinuses vibrated. Then I told them that I loved them. And they told me the same thing.

"This boyfriend," Mom asked after the tears were finally drying on all our faces. Dad had gone a little weepy too. "Is he nice? Does he treat you well?"

"Yeah, he does. I'm not really comfortable with this yet —talking about it with you guys—but he's great." Telling them the man I was seeing was Mads just was not happening today. No way could I do any more drama.

"Maybe you could talk to Brady or Jamie about him? I'm assuming they've known for some time. Parents are always the last to know." Mom sighed. Dad rubbed her shoulder. I sure had fucked up their day.

"No, neither of them knows. Just you, and Mads, and some of the Railers' team and management. Not the whole team, just the captain. I came out to Mads first. There was a fight on the ice." I tried to explain. They both got all sorts of fired-up about the slur. And that made me want to cry again, but I held back the tears. "Please don't tell Brady or Jamie. Let me do it my own way, okay?"

"Yes, of course, son," Dad hurried to say.

Mom nodded, then took a shaky sip of her tea. I'd bet they'd both have something *way* stronger than coffee or tea to drink after this talk ended.

"Tennant? Should we join GLAAD?" Dad asked.

"Oh, Bruce, I think we should," Mom gushed, like

joining GLAAD was the best thing since strawberry jam or Sir Elton John. "We can march with Tennant during Pride Week. Would you like that, Tennant?"

"That would be epic."

I honestly didn't think I could love them more than I did right then. I cried again. They did too. I was still working on getting Weepy Ten under control when I finally got myself together enough to head over to Mads' place. This was big, and I needed him.

NINE

Mads

Casey's latest text said she was fine, and sorry, but her dad, Ryker's grandfather would be the one picking him up to take him home, and that it would be before the game this weekend. She was always so organized, and strict. She'd said no to Ryker staying for the Boston game, said he needed to get home to study for tests and Ryker didn't argue. He respected his mom and even though he was disappointed about missing the game, he admitted he needed the extra studying time. Casey was a good mom, responsible in a way that I admired. She hated Ev as much as I did, although she'd had to handle him being in her life while I could get away with avoiding him.

I didn't envy her that at all.

The text had arrived at some point in the night but we'd only just woken up to it, me still on the sofa where Ryker had left me at ass o' clock this morning, and him stumbling out of the spare room rocking a serious case of bed head.

Coffee. I needed coffee, a shower, and more coffee, in that order.

Ryker's grandfather would be here in thirty if I read the text right.

"I don't know what's up with your mom, but grandpa is picking you up," I informed Ryker on a yawn, and when he didn't answer I looked at him curiously. He looked guilty, like there were a hundred secrets behind those crystal-blue eyes. "Ryker?" I asked.

He took one wide-eyed look at me and went back into his room.

It's too early for this shit. Even if it is ten thirty, it's still way too early.

I made coffee, had my shower, and still had ten minutes to spare before Ev arrived at my door. I picked up a throw cushion to tidy it, then threw it back on the floor. I wasn't changing the way I lived for Ev, and my place was clean, and homey, and mine.

Knocking on Ryker's door, I heard a muffled "come in" from inside, and pushed in. The room was his place at my place, so to speak. The posters were of the Railers, all signed, but he also had some pictures up of me and him together, and one that his mom had done of the three of us together at his fifth birthday. That day had been the very first day I was, by law, allowed anywhere near my son. A beautiful day. Hockey gear in the corner filled the room with a stale, sweaty smell, but it was one I was used to, and he was a teenage boy; their rooms stank.

A very dejected-looking Ryker sat on the edge of his bed in one of my Railers hockey jerseys. The dusky blue looked good on him, but he was pulling at the hem and unraveling the stitching.

"Wassup?" I said, and sat next to him.

"I'm sorry, Dad," he murmured, but didn't look at me.

I wasn't sure what to think of my son sitting there not

able to look me in the eye, or of the fact that he'd actually willingly called me Dad instead of his normal Jared.

"What for?"

"I told grandpa what you said, about me staying on at school, but he said I didn't need to do anything you said, and that he'd pay for everything, that I didn't need your money…" He stopped talking.

"He'd pay for what?" I asked, ignoring the whole concept of my own child not having access to my money. Twenty-five percent of everything I earned went into a fund for Ryker, not that he knew that yet, not until he was twenty-one. Of course, he'd likely be earning his own millions then, but I was the father and I was providing for my child just like I sent another twenty-five percent to Casey every month, regular as clockwork.

"CHL," he mumbled.

I couldn't hear properly. "Enough with the muttering," I snapped, because I couldn't help myself.

"The CHL," Ryker said, and this time he looked up and met my gaze and he looked absolutely torn, gutted, sad.

"Your grandpa wants you to go into the Canadian Hockey League?" I said, spelling out exactly what I knew CHL meant just to give myself time to get my head around all this.

"Grandpa says I'm being scouted and I could be playing for real up there, ready for the draft."

Temper coiled low inside me. Next time I saw Ev, I was going to kill the bastard. Of course Ryker was being scouted —he was fast and accurate, and his hockey sense was steady. Any team would be lucky to have him. But being scouted didn't mean he had to take up a place anywhere.

"We talked about this," I said as calmly as possible.

"You promised me you'd stay in school and get your diploma."

The knock on the front door was loud and demanding, and I stood up with angry words right there on the tip of my tongue. I stalked through my house and wrenched open my front door, the wood smacking back against the coat rack. Ev was standing there in a suit, looking a hundred kinds of smug. I turned away from him and he followed me in, closing the front door behind him. I thought I heard something like "nice welcome," but I didn't care one bit what the man wanted to say.

We went through the large entrance hall and into the front room. I stopped just inside the threshold of the room and let him pass.

"Is Ryker ready?" he asked as he brushed at his jacket with his hand and straightened it. "We have a meeting at twelve."

"A meeting," I said, and how the hell I kept my voice even I don't know.

"With a prospective agent who's flying out to meet us in Harrisburg," he said, and then just waited for me to say my bit. He looked like he was relishing every single moment of this.

"An agent," I repeated.

He opened his mouth to say something and I don't know, maybe I had a face like thunder, or maybe it was because I was taller, stronger, and younger than him, but he abruptly went from smug to looking concerned as I stalked him.

"Sit. Down," I said, and pointed at my sofa.

"Excuse me?"

"I am talking to my son, and you will sit out here and wait."

He made a show of looking at his watch. "I can give you five minutes."

I stepped closer. He stood his ground. One more step, and this time he moved back, almost falling over the discarded throw pillow.

"Sit. Down," I said again.

"Now listen here—"

I was right up in his face then. "You will sit yourself the fuck down and you will wait until I have goddamned finished talking to *my* son, and you will not say a fucking word."

I jabbed at his chest with my finger, and he caught my hand and twisted it. Thing was, there were only twenty years between us. He was a fit guy, an ex-hockey player, and he had moves.

But by the time I had him flailing back on the sofa with shock on his face, he knew for damn sure that this defenseman still had the strength and power to topple any kind of man.

"Now sit there and shut up, or leave," I said.

Going back into Ryker's room, I closed the door behind him and went to the window. Fresh air, even this crisp Fall air, was exactly what I needed to clear my head.

"Dad?" He sounded so incredibly lost.

I sat next to him, and pulled him in for a sideways hug. Not a bro hug, not a friends' hug, but the kind of hug that a dad gave his son. To my horror, Ryker turned and buried his face in my neck, his hair wet from his shower and his shoulders shaking. Was he crying?

Well he won't be laughing, idiot.

"Start from the beginning Ry," I said in my best gentle voice, which wasn't difficult, as the temper I'd had going on with Ev had vanished as soon as my son wanted me to comfort him.

"I told him I'd talked to you, and he said you knew nothing, that you were used up and finished, and I shouted at him, and he threatened mom, said she was weak, and it scared me, and then he said he was picking me up from yours place because whether I liked it or not I had a meeting with an agent, and now I don't know what to do."

To me, it sounded like Ryker was close to hyperventilating. I gently eased him away and wriggled back so there was room between us. He *had* been crying, his skin flushed and his eyes red.

"What do you want to do?" I asked gently. Because wasn't that what this was all about really? I had my opinions, about burn out, and Ryker growing into his body, and gaining experience and skills, and finishing his education. Ev saw Ryker as the next big thing and wanted to push him to work at it now, to be the next freaking Crosby.

That wasn't going to happen. To me, Ryker was the coolest hockey player I'd ever seen, with the most amazing skills and the ability to shoot from any part of the rink. With my pride talking, I could say he was as talented as Gretzky. But I also knew that while he was good, he wasn't the next big thing; he was a solid left wing with a future ahead of him in the NHL, but he needed to slow down and learn and grow into his height.

"I don't know what I want to do," Ryker said. "Apart from hockey. I love hockey. I want to play for the NHL. You understand that, right?"

"Yeah, you know I do. I wanted to play in the NHL more than I wanted to breathe," I said, and we exchanged wry grins.

"But you never finished school." He wasn't accusing, he just sounded like he really wanted to understand.

"That was for a very different reason, Ry. Your mom

and I, we had a battle on our hands, and I worked damn hard to get money so I could…"

That wasn't where I'd expected this to go. We'd done the whole complicated story of his conception and even hinted at some of the hurdles we'd had to jump just for me to see him. Casey and I had sat there and explained to eleven-year-old Ryker that we both loved him, that we wanted the best for him. What I never said, and I never will, is that I used up every single cent of my signing money over those years just to fight for him. Hell, I spent most of those years sleeping at friends' places or in cheap, shitty rentals. But I'd do it all again for the chance to be in Ryker's life.

"Okay, let's move this back to you, son. As I see it, your options are, you quit now and impress the scouts and get yourself up to the CHL. Or you stay at Shattuck until senior year and you're eligible for the draft but you'll have strengthened your game and grown into your height. Hell, maybe you opt to go the college route. Who knows?"

He looked uncertain for a moment, and then dipped his gaze. "I don't know what to do, Dad. Should I take what I can, when I can? What would an agent say?"

Fuck, he looked so lost, like he was pinning everything on the idea that an agent was the answer to all things. Was that what Ev had been feeding him? Agents guided and assisted, but this kind of a decision was way above the pay grade of any agent.

"Any agent who really cared about the player—and there are a lot out there, good ones—would be looking to you for what *you* want to do."

Ryker looked like he was going to cry again. Jesus, the pressure that Ev was putting on *my* son was tearing him apart from the inside out.

I moved further onto the bed, cross–legged, and waited

until he did the same thing. We used to play a game when he was a kid. I would say a word, and he would say the first thing that came into his mind. A stupid game, where every answer was related to hockey. I wished I could use that game now, but this was way more serious. I needed to string proper words together. I needed to be the adult here.

"Do you agree with your grandpa that you're the next big thing?"

I couldn't help but think of Ten as I asked that. Ten had always come high on all those lists that rated skill, and when I watched him on the ice he had a hockey sense that was rare. He was fast and confident. But under it all he was everything I wanted for Ryker—a person happy in his own skin, endlessly optimistic, when it came to hockey at least.

"No," Ryker said, and looked at me like I'd accused him of some heinous crime. "But…"

"But what? You can say anything you want. It won't go any further than this room."

"I'm good," he added with a splash of confidence I wanted to see.

"I know."

He looked right at me, with that focus I admired in him, and half smiled. "Will you be my agent?" he asked.

"God, no!" I exclaimed. I wished I hadn't said the words quite so strongly when Ryker's face fell. "I didn't mean it like that," I amended. "I'm a grunt, a player, a coach. An agent finesses all kinds of legal shit."

That made Ryker smile, and the smile reached his eyes. "Is that a technical explanation, Dad?"

"You want to go to this meeting with your grandpa?"

"No. But he won't listen to me, and he keeps saying you're wrong, and I need you to talk to me like…" He stopped, and I waited for more, because he looked so deadly serious. He bit his lip, an unfortunate habit he'd picked up from his mom. I recalled watching her biting her lip a lot the night he was conceived. One thirty-dollar room, one experimentation, and Ryker was made, just like that. Not out of love maybe, but certainly out of a strong friendship that only wavered when Casey's dad got involved.

Ryker was the best parts of me and of Casey. I couldn't be prouder of our son.

"Go on," I encouraged him. "You want me to talk like what?"

"Not my dad," he said finally, and dipped his gaze again as he flushed scarlet.

"You want me to give you advice man to man?" I smiled at him.

"No, Jesus, no." He looked aghast again, and I didn't have the heart to call him on his cursing, because hell, his mom wasn't there and he would say worse on the ice. "Properly, like hockey player to hockey player."

Now *that* I could do.

"Okay, so this is the way I see it. Looking at your skill, seeing you skate, I think you need more development time. You have a lot of raw talent, you're fast, focused, you see the puck, you look at the play not the player... it's all good." His smile was wide as I said that. "I'm so proud of the work you put in, and when I'm in the stands for your first NHL game, I will probably embarrass you by cursing the refs and shouting plays."

"Dad... jeez..."

"Look, if I were you, I would stay at Shattuck, get my education, become the left wing that can be counted on, get taller, get faster, and put myself up for the draft at eighteen, hell maybe even think about going to college and work on your skills on a college team."

"Yeah?" He looked so hopeful—settled, almost. "You think I could go to college?"

"Of course I do, hell, you're a bright kid. You could get a degree, you could do it all. College and hockey." I didn't know what college could mean to him, I hadn't gone to college, or even properly finished school, but I knew he was capable.

He glanced at the door, the confidence slipping a little. "What about grandpa?"

"I'll deal with him. And I'll talk to your mom; she and I are on the same page."

"She doesn't stand up to grandpa, though."

I remembered the day they'd slammed the door on me, Ev telling me that Casey was having an abortion. I'd seen Casey behind him, crying and saying nothing even though I called her name. I also remembered the courts, the news articles, the lies, and that singularly beautiful day when she'd turned around to her dad and said one word. He'd been mid-rant—something about me being a bad influence, drinking too much, whoring around—and she'd just said *enough*. She had a backbone that I admired, she just also knew how to keep the peace around her blustering asshole of a father.

"She would if she knew for sure what you wanted, Ry."

"Really?"

"I promise you."

"Dad? Can we talk about something else?"

Uh-oh, this sounded ominous, like there was a hidden world of hurt for me in that simple sentence.

"Yeah, sure," I said, making sure I sounded way more blasé about leading questions like that than I was. If this was a sex question, I would show some backbone and actually talk like a real adult would, about responsibility and shit. I would *not* resort to crude jokes and pass over recommendations for the best condoms.

"You could have invited him over when I was here," Ryker began. "Your new boyfriend, I mean."

For a moment I blinked at him, parsing his words, trying to get a grip on a response, but all that came out was a string of "I don't…" and "I can't…"

He shook his head sadly at me. "I left my old Railers jersey here last time and couldn't find it in the closet, so I checked the laundry in the second bathroom, because you know you never remember to empty it. I found a load of stuff in there—couple of jerseys, some boxers. They're not yours."

"They are," I lied, thinking back to when the hell I would have used the second bathroom. The only one who ever set foot in there was… shit.

"Dad," Ryker began, oh-so-freaking patiently. "Unless your name is Rowe and your number is ninety-four, then they're not yours."

"He's not… I don't…" There it went again; my capacity for rational speech was out the window.

"Then there was the text."

"What text?" This was getting worse by the minute. Ryker knowing about Ten was something I'd wanted to manage; drip-feed him the information.

"The one Ten sent about the blowjob and then signed it 'Suck you later, J,' with like twenty kisses."

Oh fuck. I was scarlet. "I didn't want you to find out this way," I said. "Ten isn't out, he's—"

"Is it good?" Ryker asked.

I balked at the question, and my dismay must have been written on my face.

Ryker snorted a laugh. "Not the sex, Dad. I meant are you and him happy? Because Mom and Martin are happy, and I want to see you the same way in your old age."

I caught the twinkle in his eye and poked at his chest. Then I sobered a little. "You think I'm too old for him?"

How the hell I thought asking my teenage son a question like that would help, I don't know, but out it came. I waited with nervous tension in my chest.

"Martin is years older than Mom," he said matter-of-factly. "Is it serious?"

"I love him," I said without thought. "We've been going slow. I want more now, but it's difficult. He's not out —you can't tell anyone."

"I wouldn't do that, but you realize if he comes out he'll be the first one to do that in the NHL? I hope that goes okay for him, because I like Ten. He has this awesome Butterfree that he evolved."

"I have no idea what you mean, but that's a good thing, right?"

"Give me your phone, Dad," Ryker asked, holding out his hand. I passed it over to him, and he typed in my code.

"How did you know my code?"

"You use my birth date, Dad," he said, with that *duh* expression only a technologically savvy teenager could muster. He clicked a few buttons, then held it still for a moment. "Okay, there you go. Pokémon."

"I don't want that on my phone—"

"Dad you have to get down with the kids like me and Ten." He couldn't help smirking.

That earned him another poke, then an out-and-out wrestle that ended up with us on the floor.

The door to Ryker's bedroom slammed open and Ev stood in the entrance. "What the hell?" he said, staring at the two of us sitting on the floor.

I glanced at Ryker, who nodded. I was supporting him,

there for him. Like the very best defenseman I could be, I had his back.

"Grandpa," he started with confidence. "I'm not getting an agent. I'm staying in school, working on my game, aiming for the draft, I might even go to college, and I'm getting Dad to run me to the airport this afternoon. I have a history paper to get done."

Ev looked like a goldfish, and I wanted to say that, but I had to stay the grown up here.

Ev crossed his hands over his chest. "I'll take this to court," he threatened, looking right at me.

Then I couldn't help it. I snorted a laugh and had to hide it behind my hand. Somehow, I'd regressed, and I wondered if the Pokémon game's influence worked that fast. When Ev didn't move, I pulled the cloak of adulthood more firmly around me and levered myself off the floor.

"I'll see you out," I said in my politest voice.

"Ryker?" Ev said, and there was a touch of anger in his voice. "You're listening to him? He's a loser who didn't even last eight years in the league."

Ryker came to stand next to me, and we bumped shoulders. "He's my dad."

Which was how it came about that we saw Ev off the property. Then we watched an old game with yours truly in fine defensive form, and drove to the airport.

The last thing my son said to me as I stood by the car was a very heartfelt, "Love you, Dad."

Sometimes simple words like that have the power to knock you to your knees. "Love you too," I called. "Play hard. Keep your head up."

"Always," he shouted, and pushed into the terminal.

I drove home with music blasting and the weight of the world lifted from my shoulders. I'd rocked that father stuff and I was the best dad in the entire world, or at least it felt that way.

I was back well before Ten was due over, and excitement filled me at the thought of telling him what Ryker and I had talked about, and also teasing him for leaving his dirty wash in my hamper.

Yes, it was serious, yes, I wanted Ten as much as breathing, and yes, I was falling completely head-over-heels in love with him. I wrote a quick text to Casey about what had happened with Ryker. She sent me back a smiley face and a simple thank you.

There was nothing to thank me for. Not really. I was just doing my job.

And now I really wanted to kiss Ten, and talk to him, and make love to him, and he couldn't get there soon enough.

Tennant

"You really don't have to knock," Mads informed me after opening the door.

I threw myself at him, plastering my lips to his, my bag hitting the floor with a dull *whump* as we staggered into the nearest wall. The door creaked shut.

Mads hefted me up tighter to him. "That was quite the greeting."

"I told them," I gasped, the kiss robbing me of breath.

He looked at me questioningly, but kept me pressed to him, his hands resting on my hips.

"My parents. I told them I was gay and they were totally okay with it!"

"Wow." His mouth hung open a bit. "That's… wow. Did you tell them about us?"

"No. Well, not really. I said there was someone, but I didn't mention names." His exhalation was huge. "I wouldn't throw you under the bus like that. You mean too much to me."

Mads buried his face in my neck, tasted the skin under my ear, then pulled back so that he could cup my face. He spent a whole minute just looking at me. My hands moved up and down his arms.

"I'd really like to make love to you"

"I'd really like to be inside you."

My first thought was to pump the air and hoot, "Finally!" I bit that reaction back.

"I would love that so much."

Mads picked up my bag, then offered me his hand. For some reason, after all the time spent pitching myself around because of lack of sex, now that he was waiting for me to take his hand to actually go have sex, I was feeling stupid and shy.

He arched a brow. "If you're not ready, Ten, that's fine."

"No, I'm ready." I placed my hand in his. My heart started dancing irregularly. "Are you kidding? I've been ready for weeks. Months."

"There's a difference between being physically ready and mentally ready." We stood in his tidy living room—which had all kinds of furnishings—holding hands while he tried to feel me out. "Are you sure you're mentally ready?"

"I'm sure." I stepped up to him and kissed him with all I had, our clasped hands pinned between his chest and mine. When we broke apart, I found his gaze resting on me. "I'm so sure. I want you inside me."

"Dear God, Tennant."

He sighed, took a light kiss, then led me to his bedroom. It was a nice room. Filled with a dresser and a bed. I'd been in it at least two dozen times, but now that we were getting down to more than humping each other or touching each other's dicks through our underwear, the room seemed bigger, the bed enormous. Hell, my lover suddenly seemed to have grown a foot or two.

"You look like you're ready to run," he said.

"I'm feeling stupid and small."

He released my hand, then placed my overnight bag beside the light oak dresser.

"Okay, so I've sucked lots of dick, right?" My nerves were jangling. Mads nodded. "So, I'm good with that. But the other stuff…"

"Tennant, there's no rule that says we have to have anal sex."

"No, see, I want to, but the last time it kind of went badly. It hurt, and he was a fumbling moron like I was. See, I want this to be perfect for you."

"And it will be. Why don't we just see where our passion takes us?" He pulled off his Railers T-shirt and let it drop to the floor, then he unzipped the old jeans he'd been wearing. They slipped down to his ankles, along with his boxers. Dear God, there was so much Mads. His body was hard and lean, bigger than mine in just about every way. He let me look at him for as long as I needed.

I rushed to peel off my clothes, then felt a little inadequate in comparison to him. His cock was so rugged and male. Thick and long and uncut, hard, and weepy with fat veins. And then there was mine, which up to that point I'd thought was pretty damn impressive.

"By God, you are so beautiful," he said, which made me flush. "Look at that. I didn't think Tennant Rowe knew how to blush. It looks good on you."

My feelings were all over the place. I suddenly felt like a kid. Like some stupid kid who was finally where he wanted to be and was just realizing that he was in over his head.

"Can you come touch me, please?" I asked, hoping that wasn't too weak a request.

"I'd love to." He padded over to me, his gaze staying

with mine. "Why don't you tell me what you want, Tennant?"

"You," I managed to croak, my fingertips crying out to reach out and touch him. "I want you to touch me everywhere. Kiss me everywhere. Then I want you inside me."

"Are you sure?"

Mads took that last step—the one that pressed his nude body to mine. His prick nestled against mine. I whimpered a bit. He slid a hand around me, pulled me flush to him, and lowered his head to kiss my neck. My head fell back, my eyes slid shut, and my body became his to do with as he wanted.

"Are you sure, Tennant?"

"Yes, yes, I'm sure."

He put a few soft bites along my throat, then eased me back onto the bed, his weight settling on top of me. He felt perfect. Strong and long, firm with sharp planes and rolling muscles under my fingers. I wrapped around him like one of those flowery, clingy vines Mom planted by the lamp post in the back yard. Mads kissed me. I blossomed under his mouth and hands. All this time I'd thought I was so experienced and such a top-notch lover, but Mads showed me that making love to someone was vastly different from simply fucking someone.

He was so gentle, so patient, easing me into lying back in his arms as he stroked me and petted me, kissed my chest and toyed with my ass.

"If you want me to stop, just say so," he repeated while working me into a lather. By the time he was pressing a finger into me, I was beyond speech. Animalistic sounds and grunts were all that came out of me. He worked that slippery finger in while dropping kisses along my cheek and eye. "How are you?"

"Great. Ah, man, that is amazing." I groaned, then shivered, my fingers twisted in the bedding.

"Good, good." He stole a kiss, then pulled that finger out. I arched up, eager for more. "This is going to be even better." He pushed two fingers in, then began rotating them, pressing them deep, scissoring them, and bumping my prostate. "Shhh, shhh," he whispered as I thrashed around wildly, my balls tightening up. The fingering stalled as I slithered back from the edge.

"I'm so close, Mads… so close. I want to come with you inside me…"

"Let's take our time."

"Seriously, I'm hearing that now?"

He chuckled, kissed me lightly, then licked and nibbled his way down to my cock. Arm over my stomach, he sucked me deeply into his mouth while cupping my balls. I bucked up, eager to get all of myself down his throat. He pressed my ass back onto the bed, then started sucking hard and fast. His tongue swirled over the tip, then he took me deep. There was no holding back. No way could I stop the orgasm that ran me over. Mads let the head of my cock rest on his tongue, his fingers fisted at the base. I pounded on the mattress. He lapped up every droplet that rested on his lips and fingers.

"You're tastier than I imagined," he growled while giving my cock a final stroke.

I was still quaking when he shifted around, rolling away from me. I touched him all over. His back, his arms, his hip, his stomach. Sitting up, I wiggled closer to his back, rubbing my hands over his shoulders while kissing the nape of his thick neck. His skin broke into gooseflesh, which made me smile. When he moved to face me, I skittered back onto the bed, my gaze dropping to his latex-covered cock. When I reached for him, he didn't stop me. His prick was smooth and hard in my hand. I fell onto my back, guiding him up and over me, squeezing my fingers tightly around him.

Mads settled between my legs, easing my thighs up until they rested on my chest. All the while his eyes glowed like he'd been given a rare prize or something.

"Are you sure about this?" His grip on my knees was firm but not painful.

I nodded as I worked to calm my breathing a little. "Mads, I swear I'm fine. If you pull back now, I'll go freaking insane. Please, I want you in me. *Please.*"

He leaned down to get a kiss, the tip of him nudging at my opening. "Relax, Ten," he purred before pushing his cock in a bit.

The burn was familiar. I winced.

He paused. "You okay? Any time this gets to be too much, say so."

"More," I huffed, and dug at his biceps.

He gave me more and even more, inch by inch, easing me into the possession, giving my body time to stretch and adjust.

"I can't breathe," I panted when he leaned in to my legs. "Fuck, it's…"

"Yes, it really is." He flicked his hips quickly. I bowed up off the bed. "You good?"

"Oh, fuck yes," I replied, my fingers slipping along the surface of his sweaty skin. "Give me more, Mads."

We found a rhythm. It was tentative at first, easy. Then it increased, picking up speed. I held on to his arms, my gaze pinned to Mads as he filled me then withdrew, each stroke moving me across the bed an inch or so. I asked him for more again. He gave me more speed, more depth, more gyrating hip action. My head slid off the side of the mattress. He yanked me back onto the bed without losing his pace. My legs were cramping. The bed seconded our tempo, hitting the wall with a rapid *bang-bang-bang*.

"Ten, shit, Ten," he growled.

I wrapped my fingers around his forearms as he came. He dug into the mattress with his knees, pushing himself up and deeper on the come stroke. His muscles constricted, his jaw locked, and his cock kicked deep inside me. He was the most the stunning man I'd ever seen, and that was all I could think as I was coming.

He was beautiful. And he was mine.

Clawing like a cat, I writhed under him, his depth painful and pleasurable at the same time.

"Sorry, shit… sorry, Ten," he huffed, and eased out of me. My leg muscles tightened up. I rolled to my side to work the cramps out of my thighs. "I'm sorry." He ran a hand over my side then up my back.

"No, it's good, it's just thigh cramps." I groaned.

He lay down behind me, pulled me close to him, and licked the tattoo on the back of my neck. His hands traveled down my side to my hip and then to my thigh. His fingers worked the oxygen-starved muscles. I moaned and sighed as the cramps eased up.

"You okay now?" His words were hot little puffs on my inkwork. I turned to pudding, melting back into him as he massaged my thigh. "Are you sure it was just cramps?"

"Yeah, it was just cramps. You were super gentle."

I rolled my head to the left and got a sloppy kiss. His hand came up to rest on my stomach as his tongue danced over mine. We lay there for a long time, kissing, and touching. I rolled over to face him.

"That was worth the wait."

"Glad to hear it. I have to take care of this condom."

He pressed a kiss to my forehead, then slipped from the knotted bedding. I thought about getting up to get a drink, but my legs ached and my ass was tender. No way was I letting him see me gimping around, so I pulled the coverlet up and closed my eyes, inhaling the scent of me, Mads, and sex on the air.

"Hey, here."

I swam through the fog of post-sex sleep. Mads was sitting beside me on the bed with a bottle of spring water and wearing a smug smile.

"Drink all of it."

I sat up. The cover slithered down my chest and puddled on my lap.

"Thanks."

"Do you need anything else?" He was so attentive. It was so cute. I shook my head while I sucked down twenty ounces. "I have all kinds of food."

I tossed the empty bottle onto the floor and reached for him, my hand coming to rest on his shoulder. I pulled his mouth to mine.

"I want more of you," I told him, gave him a shove that sent him tumbling back to the mattress, then eyed his limp cock hungrily. "Yeah, more of you will do just fine."

Lucky me, he was willing to give me all the Mads I could handle.

THE INSIDE OF MADS' fridge looked like my parents'. It was packed full of food. Good food. Milk, eggs, fruit, and fresh vegetables. Yogurt and juice bottles. Sports drinks and bottled water with added vitamins and minerals. So the total opposite of my fridge, which had half a pizza still in the box, a jug with an inch of sour milk in the bottom, and a bottle of ketchup. Oh yeah, and a six-pack of Miller Lite that now held only one unopened bottle. I really needed to do some shopping.

My stomach snarled, reminding me of the fact that I had expended some major energy last night. I grabbed the bottle of orange juice and a container of strawberries, then hip-checked the door closed. Knowing I had also lost some fluid in Mads' bed, I opened the carton and took a long drink. It was unsweetened and pulpy, the fleshy bits of orange sticking to my teeth. I needed a toothbrush and shower in the worst way. A grumble from my gut reminded me that food was number one on the priority list.

I rummaged around in his cupboards, sipping OJ all the while, until I found a bowl. The silence of his place started to wear on my nerves, so I pulled my phone out of the back pocket of my jeans, opened Spotify, and found a playlist that appealed. Now that I had some Glass Animals playing, I could think better. Growing up in a house with three boys meant noise. Lots of noise and lots of junk scattered around. Places like this, all soundproofed and tidy, set me on edge.

The tiles were cool under my bare feet as I padded to the sink and washed the fat, red berries by holding the container under the flow of water. Mom always said to wash your fruit, but a rinse should suffice. I was too hungry to dick around with anything else. I plucked a huge strawberry out and bit it off by the leafy stem. The berry was ripe, filled with sweet red juice that coated my tongue.

"Oh man," I sighed, then went for another.

I'd polished off about a third of the container when his arms curled around my middle, startling me so badly I fumbled the berry that was close to my mouth. Mads ran his tongue over my tattoo, sending a spear of red-hot lust to my groin. His hands flattened over my bare stomach. I smiled as he rubbed a small circle over my abdomen.

"What is this shit playing on your phone?"

"Seriously? You don't know Glass Animals?"

I looked back to find his blue eyes on me. I held up a berry for him to eat over my shoulder. His teeth were white and even as he gently bit the fruit. Juice ran over my fingers, dripping to the bare skin of my shoulder. I dropped the stem. It rolled down my chest. He ran the tip of his tongue over my fingertips, and then sucked my index finger into his mouth. My cock began to plump up. Between his sucking on my finger and his hands roaming down into the waistband of my jeans, I was pretty much a goner.

"And you have a Pokémon tattoo on the back of your neck."

"That's your comeback for everything. It's lame and old, like you." I leaned back into him, his erection pressing against my ass. "Which tastes better? My fingers or my neck?"

"Are you being coy, Tennant?"

I shrugged, since I wasn't sure what being coy really meant.

"I haven't found a part of you that tastes bad yet."

That was when I turned around in his arms, shoved my fingers into his short blond hair, and kissed him as deeply as I could. His tongue slipped over mine. He pushed his hand down into my jeans, his fingers skimming over the tender head of my cock. A rolling shudder broke free, branching out from my core to my arms, legs, hands, and feet. When his fingers coiled around my cock, I gasped, breaking the wet seal of our lips.

"I thought a dude your age would need a day or two to recover... Ah man, that is so good." He stroked me from base to tip while nipping along my jaw line. His tongue ran up over my cheek.

"You've got one hell of a beard for a kid your age," he

purred, then pressed a soft kiss to the corner of my eye. Keeping upright was growing tricky. My knees felt soft.

"I'm not a kid," I reminded him with more than a little attitude. He pulled back an inch or so and thumbed the head of my cock. A ragged breath fluttered over my lips.

"No, you are certainly *not* a kid. Sorry for that."

He dipped into my mouth gently, teasing me with flicks of his tongue along the edge of my teeth, all the while working my cock with a tight fist. Just as I was falling into the pace of his strokes, he stopped. Once his hand was out of my jeans, he found my fly.

"Not a kid at all," he stated before freeing my cock and dropping to his knees in front of me.

"Oh shit," I gasped when he sucked me into his mouth.

Fingers seeking purchase, I found the edge of the counter after knocking the container of strawberries to the floor. Mads closed his eyes and went deep, slipping my cock down his throat as his fingers held my ass cheeks. My jeans lingered around my knees. He seemed content to leave them there, his head bobbing as he twisted and twirled his tongue along the bottom of my cock. The man knew how to give head. Like, he had escort skills, or what I assumed an escort would know. I'd never used one. If I had, he'd have looked just like Mads, who was in control of his maturity and sexual experience. He worked it so well...

"Are you close?"

I grunted and thrust, the rasp of his teeth along my cock painful but not enough to pull me back from the brink. Mads cupped my balls, squeezed firmly, then went back down on me. One hand on my stomach to keep me in place, he sucked and clasped, sucked and clasped, until I blew apart. My head kicked back violently, his name falling out of me as I came. He swallowed rapidly, humming in pleasure as I bucked and moaned.

"Oh, oh, oh shit, shit." My balls contracted in his grip.

Mads licked me clean, then got to his feet. His eyes were like pools of blue fire.

"You want me to suck you off?" I asked.

"No, I want you to pick up the berries, wash them off, and bring them back to bed." He padded off, giving me a great view of his tight ass and corded thighs.

I pulled up my jeans, zipped, and scooped up and washed strawberries as fast as I could. I ran to the bedroom, a dripping plastic container full of freshly rinsed berries in my hand. Mads was spread out across his bed, filling the thing with hard muscle, long limbs, and a thick, hard cock and heavy balls. I couldn't tear my gaze from his prick. You'd think I would have gotten enough of him last night, but that didn't seem to be the case.

"Good man. Now bring them over here." He patted the mattress beside him, his lush mouth quirked up into a wicked smile.

"What are we going to do with them?" I wasn't sure why I even cared. Right then, I couldn't think of anything he could do with a berry that I'd protest him doing.

"Nothing that you won't love."

"Yeah?"

"Yeah. Now bring them over here and lie down with me."

I crossed the room, kicked the knotted covers on the floor aside, and placed one knee then the other onto the mattress. The bottom sheet was all screwed up, baring the far corner of the mattress by Mads' head. He took the container, ignoring the droplets of water falling onto the sheet and his stomach. I couldn't ignore them, though. I bent down and lapped them off, enjoying the feel of his skin twitching as my tongue roamed over it.

"Hold that over your abs," I told him, and he did. "Shake it."

Water escaped through the air holes, dotting his abdomen. I threw an arm over his chest, then went to work, licking and chasing each drop of water. He made deep, heady noises as I cleaned him up. I'd almost worked my way to his cock when his fingers slid into my hair and pulled me gently upward.

"Once you get something in your mind…"

He flipped the container open and plucked out a fat berry. I tossed a leg over him and seated myself on his thighs. My gaze fell to his cock.

"Hey," he called, and I glanced up at him. "My eyes are up here," he teased, then fed me the berry. I chewed and swallowed.

"But your dick is here." I ran the back of a finger over the velvety shaft. "And I'm much more interested in your dick than your eyes at the moment. Sorry. Totally shallow, I know."

"Totally male."

He chuckled before choosing another berry. This one he placed on his chest, taking time to lay it just so that it didn't roll off his nipple. I liked this game already. I leaned over him, trapping that fat, hot cock of his between us, then lifted the strawberry from his skin with my tongue, making sure I got a nice lap of his tight little nipple as I did. He sighed roughly. Another berry came to rest on his other nipple. A smaller one. I grabbed that one with my teeth, chewed quickly, swallowed, then flicked his nipple with the tip of my tongue. My cock was slowly fattening up. Mads' prick was like a branding iron pushed into my belly.

"Can you fuck me again?" I asked while mouthing his nipple.

"Patience," he said.

He gave me a soft berry to focus on. It was super ripe. I smashed it against the roof of my mouth. He reached for me, pulled me down, and licked at my closed mouth, seeking entrance. I opened for him, shared the juice and the flesh, the sticky sweetness, then smeared it all over his lips and chin with my tongue. His hold on the back of my head grew firmer as we sucked on each other's lips and tongues. Then he rolled me onto my back.

"Fuck, yeah," I groaned, eager as hell to get him inside me. I brought up my legs, but he pushed them back down.

"Patience," he said yet again, lowering himself over me, stealing a kiss as he pumped his cock against my ass.

"Fucker," I growled playfully. "Tell a man to be patient, then you perpetrate that kind of tease?"

"You need to learn that it's not always about shoving your dick into the first available orifice." He ran rough palms up over my arms, pinning my hands by the headboard, all while trailing kisses along my jaw.

"It kind of is." I arched up, crazy mad to get him buried inside me again. He held me down, licked and sucked, nibbled and gnawed on my throat and mouth until I thought I'd go insane. "Mads, come on! Fuck's sake, I'm dying here."

"Tennant, you already came once. You'll be fine."

Oh, right. I *had* blown a wad back in the kitchen. That was where the berries had come from. And Mads hadn't come yet this morning. Dude must have a killer case of blue balls.

"Just enjoy the play."

"Right, enjoy the play."

I wiggled under him, hoping to entice him to penetrate me. I mean, his cock was resting *right* against my ass. One flick and he'd be inside me. He released my wrists and sat back, rolling his hips so that his prick now lay by the base of my cock. I looked down to see his cock resting on the dark curls, a sparkling drip of precum leaking from him.

"Mads, let me get to your dick," I begged, but no, the shit grabbed the stupid berries and picked another ripe one from the container.

"You know what I'm going to do with this?"

"Make a fruit frappe?" I reached for his cock. He gently slapped my hand to the side.

"No, I'm going to do this with it."

He smashed the fruit against my chest, smearing the pulp into the dark circlet of my left nipple. Then he sucked it clean. He suckled hard, pulling the little bud into his mouth, then grazing it with his sharp teeth. I yelped in pleasure, dug my heels into the bedding, and grasped at his bare back.

"Want me to do it to the other one?"

"Yes, yes, shit yes." The words exploded out of me in brisk, short pants.

Mads took his time with the berry shit, crushing strawberry after strawberry against my flesh, first my chest, then my chin, then down to my navel, which he tongued madly.

"Ah, Christ, shit, damn, fucking hell I can't… Ah, Mads, shit, man…"

"Yeah, you're close," he mumbled, his fingers working two stout berries into a fine paste. "I want you to hug your knees to your chest, okay?"

He didn't have to ask twice. Our gazes met and held. "Are you going to lick that off my taint?"

"And a few other places. You're going to come for me while I do it, and no dick will penetrate any ass."

I groaned so long and so hard that Mads chuckled. The smile left his face when his fingers found my ass. He worked the berry paste into me in slow, sweet, torturous ways. One finger and then two, in and then out, up over my balls and then back down. His tongue dipped into me, swirled over and around my entrance. His prediction was right. I did come for him as he rimmed me, and all he had had to do was grab my dick and squeeze it hard one time.

"See," he said as he settled close, the tops of his thighs resting against my ass cheeks, my knees still tight to my chest. "No dick in ass."

He placed my hand on his cock and showed me how he liked to be worked. I stretched out my legs, hooking them over his shoulders. His gaze locked with mine and he came hard and fast, hot spunk coating my fingers, chest, and stomach. He was beautiful during his orgasm. I could fall in love with him so easily.

"Sweet Jesus," he panted as I milked him. "You're such a pretty man."

He huffed as the afterglow of his release began to settle on his broad back. He dropped to one side, hands fisted on either side of my head, and kissed me sweetly, rolling his tongue over mine in slow, gentle strokes.

"I think I have berries stuck to my back," I told him as he swung himself from the bed a short while later.

"Yeah, the bed is now a fruit salad," he replied.

"Ha ha, funny man."

I stretched like an old cat in a new sunbeam, fingers touching the headboard and toes tickling the footboard. I felt Mads' eyes on me, so I rolled my hips a bit and got the appreciative groan I'd been hoping for.

"I'M GOING to wash up. Stay put—I'll bring you a washcloth."

"Cool."

Off he went into the master bath. I rolled around for a

bit, then jumped up. Yep, there were berries all over the place. On the floor, on the bed. Some had been smashed into the mattress where the sheet had been pulled off. Jared turned the water on in the bathroom. I found the container and started picking up the non-flattened berries from the floor and bedding. His doorbell rang.

"Mads, someone's at the door. Want me to see who it is?" I shouted, and tossed the berry basket onto the dresser.

"Probably the paper boy. I keep cash on the side table by the front door." He peeked around the door, soapy washcloth pressed to his chest. "Pay the kid and come back so I can wash the big chunks off your backside." He waggled a brow, then ducked back into the bathroom.

I found my jeans in record time and hauled them up over my ass. The bell ringing turned into banging.

"Shit, okay, keep your fucking cap on, kid," I shouted as I jogged and zipped. I dug at a sticky berry that had gotten smashed between my shoulder blades with one hand as I ripped the front door open with my other. "What does he owe you for?"

"Tennant?" Brady asked in a squeaky kind of stunned voice.

Words slammed around inside my skull but none would come out.

"What the fuck is going on here?"

"Ten, did you find the money on the side table?" Mads shouted, then walked out into the living room with a towel tied around his waist. His eyes flared in surprise, but his voice was cool and calm. "Brady."

"You motherfucker," Brady snarled.

He threw his overnighter to the floor and went after Mads like an incensed wolf. The two big defensemen collided like a couple of semis. Mads' bare back slammed against the wall. The portrait of the Madsen family bounced off its nail and hit the floor, the frame breaking, which allowed the glass to fall out. I dove at the two of them, trying to break them up before any of the punches that my fucked-up brother was throwing landed. Too late, sadly. Brady got a clean right hook around Mads' beefy forearms. The man would have a hell of a shiner tomorrow. I shoved and tugged at Brady, my arm finally snaking around his throat, the only thing that seemingly cut into his rage. Not being able to breathe will cool your ass down. I hung off him like a lemur, the sleeper hold Jamie had taught me all those years ago finally being executed properly.

"Get…off…me," Brady gasped as we spun around in circles.

We knocked over an end table, broke a lamp, and upended the recliner, but I finally got him away from Mads. I released the sleeper and danced in front of my brother, putting a hand to his heaving chest.

"I will fucking *kill* you! What are you doing with my little brother?" Brady bellowed around me.

"Hey, asshole, it's a consensual adult relationship." I got both hands on his chest, fingers resting on his nice suit jacket, and shoved. Hard. He stumbled back a step or two, gawking at me as if he'd just really seen me for the first time. "I'm twenty-fucking-two years old!"

"And he's the same age as me!" Brady shouted with a jerky wave at Mads.

"Brady, I know this wasn't the best way for you to find out, but—" Mads tried to say.

"No! You do *not* get to talk about this, *Mads.*" Brady shook a finger at my lover. "You're supposed to be a friend. Friends don't fuck other friends' baby brothers."

"I'm not your baby brother anymore, Brady. Fuck's sake, I'm a man!" I shouted as loudly as I could. Hopefully the whole city would hear how tired I was of being thought of as a child all the time by my brothers. "I'm a man who picks who he sleeps with. I picked Mads. Deal or leave, but there will be no more fists."

The room was as still and silent as outer space. I stood between my older brother and Mads, arms dangling at my sides, muscles coiled in case I had to choke Brady down again. He reached up to rub at his throat.

"Since when are you gay?" Brady asked, his voice softer now, weak, thick with emotion and confusion.

"Since forever." I glanced back at Mads standing his ground as his left eye watered.

"Jesus, Mom and Dad are going to flip when they find out," my brother muttered.

"They already know. And they acted *way* better than you did."

Brady could not have been more shocked if he'd been holding bare wires in his hands.

"Maybe I should leave you two alone to talk." Mads slipped around us into the kitchen, probably to find some ice or a bag of frozen peas for that eye.

"You told Mom and Dad before me?" Brady seemed to be genuinely stunned and hurt.

"Well, duh." That was my reply. Brady's face screwed up with irritation. "I knew you and Jamie would be assholes when you found out. Well, you'd be an asshole. Jamie would probably just be Jamie."

His shoulders caved in. "You're gay. Shit, I never saw it."

"That's because you never looked. You were too busy trying to run my fucking life, tell me who to date and what team to play on, how to dress and what music to listen to. Did you ever just once stop trying to be the boss of the world and ask me how I felt about any of the decrees and judgments you passed down from on high?"

He rubbed absently at his throat, his eyes lackluster. "No, I guess I never did."

"Then why the hell would I have told you? Mom and Dad were cool. Shit, the team is more accepting than you are."

"The team knows?"

I shrugged. They had to know right? If the captain had figured it out, surely the rest of the team wouldn't be far behind.

His hand fell from his throat. "They know about you and Mads?"

"No, not that, but they probably all know I'm gay."

"Christ, you told strangers before you told your own brother?" He sat down hard. Good thing the sofa was behind him, or his ass would have dropped to the floor. "Does Jamie know?"

"I didn't tell the team and no, I haven't told Jamie yet. I was going to tell him when we played down in Florida next week."

"When were you going to tell me?"

I had no answer for that one.

Brady blew out a long breath, and then buried his face in his hands. "You weren't going to tell me, were you?"

"Eventually, yeah, because I'd have to." I walked over and picked up the broken picture before someone stepped on the square of glass.

"Christ. Do you hate me that much?"

I glanced over at him from where I was crouching. He'd dropped his hands. His dark eyes were dewy. Shit. Was he going to cry? I put a knee on the floor while hugging the busted frame that had held a nice shot of Mads and Ryker.

"It's not that I hate you. I mean, you're my brother… I love you. But you're such an elitist prick all the time."

His dark head snapped up at that comment.

"You are. You've done nothing but talk down to me about every fucking decision I've ever made." I stood up and placed the broken picture on the end table. Then I righted the recliner.

"I was only trying to make sure you didn't make stupid mistakes, Tennant."

"Maybe I *need* to make those mistakes, Brady." I sat down in the chair I'd just gotten back on its feet. "Maybe you need to let me make mistakes."

"But why would you want to screw up your chances of being the next big name in hockey? You've got the talent. Way more than Jamie or I could ever hope to have. Why come to Harrisburg? Christ, why hook up with one of your coaches?" He scrubbed at his face with both hands, and then threw a look at me. "When the team finds out about you two, it's going to be a mess. Why would you choose Mads, of all people?"

"I didn't choose him, it just happened. Love just happens."

Okay. Uh wow. Let's put this buggy into reverse, Tennant. Love? Really? Shit. Yes. Love. All sorts of love.

"I love him." That sounded funny—wobbly, and kind of shaky—but man did it feel right. "And if we go down in flames because of us, then we go down in flames. I'm willing to take that risk to be with him."

Brady stared at me forever. "When did you grow up?"

I snorted at the comment. "I'm not sure I have yet, but I'm working on it. But see, I have to do it *by myself*. I have to make my life decisions. I have to fuck up and I have to figure out how to fix the fuck-ups. You or Jamie can't do it for me. So back the fuck off and let me live my life. You live yours."

"I'd say you've done a lot of growing up over the past few months," he murmured, then glanced in the direction where Mads had gone. "Are you sure it has to be Mads?"

"Yep, I am totally positive it has to be Mads."

"Right. And I need to apologize to him, yeah?"

"Oh *hell* yeah," I said, then jerked my head in the direction of the kitchen. "Why don't you go try to do that? I'll clean up this mess."

"You know I boss you around because I love you, right?"

"I know. You can't help it that you're an overbearing idiot. Eldest child and all that. Go talk to Mads."

Brady gathered himself up, unknotted his tie, shoved it into the back pocket of his trousers, and walked into the kitchen to face Mads.

I fell back into the recliner, stared up at the ceiling, and tried to come to grips with the knowledge that I'd fallen insanely in love with Jared Madsen.

ELEVEN

Mads

I heard every single word, but then it was easy, because they were shouting so loud that people on the next street could probably hear them.

Love just happens. That was what Ten said to Brady. He said he loved me, that he was *in love* with me. The words were equal parts stunning and overwhelming. Because what happened when two people were in love with each other? That was more than just sex; it was hearts and flowers and promises.

God, I'm so fucking scared.

The shouting lessened and became more like serious conversation. I moved into the small laundry area I had and found some of my sweats, feeling less vulnerable than just being in a towel. I immediately turned to the coffee machine, pulling it apart bit by bit, because clearly it was vitally important that I clean it today. My face hurt where Brady had gotten in the punch of a freaking life-time. I didn't think he'd broken anything, but I had to dig deep into my hockey reserves to ignore the pain. There was no way I was standing in the kitchen with an ice pack on my face; I was not giving Brady the satisfaction.

"Mads?" Brady asked from behind me.

I dunked the filter holder into the hot soapy water in the sink and held it under for a while.

"Brady," I murmured in reply, but didn't turn to face him.

"Sorry for hitting you, dude," he offered in what seemed to me like the most insincere way ever. It was on the same level as, "Shit, sorry I picked up your water bottle by mistake."

I let go of the machine part and it bobbed to the surface, a stream of bubbles flowing from it. I may have overdone the dish detergent a little.

"Doesn't matter," I said, because it didn't matter. What was important was that Brady and his brother weren't at odds with each other, and that Brady would now treat Ten a little differently after their talk.

And then came the interrogation.

"Did you always know he was gay, from when we were kids?" Brady asked, cautiously.

I didn't like that question at all. Was he saying that because I was bi I must have a fully functioning gaydar and must have known? Ten would only have been twelve when I spent time with Brady in the minors—hell, he'd been a kid and probably hadn't known for certain whether he was gay or straight or anywhere else on the spectrum.

Whatever Brady meant to achieve with the query, it came over as an accusation. I grabbed a dish towel and the machine part and dried it and my hands, and finally I turned away from the sink to look at Brady. He winced as he saw my face. I hadn't managed to get a shot at him, not a real one, and part of me wanted to punch him right then just to get him to back the fuck off with the questions.

"No. I'm damn sure he didn't even know himself, and I don't have magic fucking gaydar. I didn't even know until he freaking told me, which for your information was only a couple months back. So don't even start accusing me of keeping secrets."

Brady's face fell. I was right—he had been accusing me of hiding the truth. The part of me that wanted to punch him was back with a vengeance. Then he said something that knocked back my anger and turned the whole situation on its head.

"Shit," he began. "I was hoping he hadn't gone through everything alone; that he'd at least had someone to talk to."

My chest tightened. Brady was looking at me like he'd just lost game seven in the Cup finals. Devastated.

"Brady—"

"What does it mean for him?" Brady asked me, and he sat heavily on one of the stools, his elbows on the counter.

I wanted to say something to make things right at that point, some glib comment about how Ten was a strong guy and how it wasn't *that bad* for a player to be different on a team. The Railers were full of all kinds of guys, split fairly equally between American, Canadian and European; that much was a given. Cultural differences began there, and that was just the start of all their differences. I wasn't naive enough to align sexual preference with something like the province a guy was born in, but I hoped that the team discovering Ten was gay wouldn't matter in the grand scheme of things. Particularly when the team was cohesive and on a tear to win a game.

"There was that kid in college, the one who came out," Brady said. "He's been getting all this hate mail—threats, even."

I'd read about that, sent a quick email of support to

him, but he wasn't a player with the same skillset as Ten. He wasn't the one making it into the NHL and having a spotlight on him. It could be a million times worse for Ten. Then it hit me how badly I was trivializing what any guy in hockey was going through if they were gay.

"The Railers are supportive," I said.

"And he has you," Brady said.

I hadn't even made sense of how I was feeling, but Brady looked like he wanted an answer.

"I will always have his back," I offered.

Brady considered my words. "If you hurt him—"

"You'll kill me, I know. Well, you can try…"

"Fuck you, Mads," Brady said without heat. "I could take you any day."

"Fuck you back."

Brady scrubbed his eyes. He looked like the weight of the world was on his shoulders, as only the captain of an NHL team can.

"Mom and Dad were okay?" he asked me softly.

Ten answered from his position in the doorway. How long he'd been standing there, I didn't know. "Did you expect them not to be?" he asked.

He had his cell phone in his hand and he looked different somehow. Confident, maybe. Was that just because I was in love with him? Was I just praying Ten would stay confident, positive, and not give in to any kind of hate thrown his way? However hard management tried, there could be signs at games, slurs, hate, articles, questions about his abilities as an athlete. I'd seen it all at one level or another.

I'd also known other hockey players who loved men, who fucked men—Jesus, one guy in LA was living with his boyfriend. The team spun it as roommates, but a lot of people knew the real story. Ten didn't have to come out publicly. He could play hockey until he was forty, and whatever relationships he had could be kept on the down-low.

Ten was asking a good question. Bruce and Jean Rowe were good parents, with a broad outlook on life. Had Brady expected them to be different when faced with one of their sons coming out?

"No," Brady said immediately, but he didn't sound so sure.

"Mum wants to join support groups and march in Pride with me."

Brady blinked at him, probably considering whether Ten was fucking with him. Also, the whole thing about a Pride parade meant Ten would be out and proud and everyone would know he was gay. I could almost pinpoint the moment when Brady had to stop himself hyperventilating, and the moment where he pulled his shit together.

"I'll march with you," he announced.

Ten went over to his brother, bumped arms, then gave him the biggest noogie, Brady cursing up a storm. "I'll hold you to that," Ten said. Then he looked at me and I saw his smile, the heat in his eyes, and I couldn't help but smile back.

"Jesus, Mads, stop eye-fucking my little brother," Brady muttered.

For that he got a smack on the back of his head from Ten, and they bickered for a short while. I left them to it, turning back to my super-important cleaning-of-the-coffee-machine job. I would do that for a while, then make an excuse to go hide in my room; give the brothers their space. They needed that. But it seemed Ten had other ideas, placing his cell on the counter next to me and thumbing through his contacts to Jamie's number.

"Will you stay?" he asked quietly as the sound of the call connecting filled the room.

I had maybe seconds to answer, but this was important to Ten. If he was telling Jamie, then there was nowhere else I wanted to be than right there next to him.

"I'm not going anywhere," I said, a little gruffly because my throat felt tight with emotion.

"Yo, Ten," Jamie answered. His voice echoed a little, like maybe he was at the rink. I knew Jamie was playing today, an evening game, not a matinee like us. Talking of which, we only had a couple of hours to get to the rink, and Ten really still needed a shower; he smelled of berries and sunshine and I wanted to kiss him all over, and I couldn't do that at work.

"Jamie, hey."

"Won't work," said another voice, a deep Russian-accented voice, "not throw game for you, Little-Rowe."

There was some scuffling and cursing, and a very resounding, "Give me back my fucking phone, asshole." And then Jamie was back. "Fucking Russian goalies," he muttered. "Wassup, Ten. You okay?"

That was Jamie's default setting—he always started conversations wanting to know if everything was okay with the person he was talking to. Because if it wasn't, then it was a given that Jamie would have a solution to your issues.

Solve this, Jamie, I thought. *Your little brother is gay and sleeping with a guy older than him, and oh yeah, he plays professional sports for a living.*

"Look I have something to tell you. I wanted to—"

"Oh shit, Ten, did the fucking Railers trade you? What the hell? Fuckers. Tell me you got sent somewhere good."

I bristled at the insinuation. What was it with Ten's brothers and their anti-Railers bullshit? One day we'd lift the

Stanley Cup, and then they'd be crying into their beers. I realized I'd gone off on a tangent in my thoughts when Ten's voice could be heard saying more or less the same thing. He rounded it off by calling both his brothers fucking idiots.

I tended to agree. The Railers were a new team, but we had depth, and we were going to rock this league so hard they wouldn't know what hit them. I was going to take great pleasure in watching my team take down both Boston and Florida, then taking Brady and Jamie out for dinner somewhere way too expensive and making them pay.

"My bad," Jamie said, his voice less echoing. The noise of others in the background had faded a little, but he was still with other guys. "So, the Railers didn't trade you…" He trailed away expectantly.

"Look, I didn't want to do this over the phone," Ten began, looking to me for support.

I placed a hand over his, and caught the approval in Brady's expression. Yay me, I'd finally done something right.

"Do what, Ten? Jesus, kid, you're freaking me out," Jamie said. "Wait, I'm taking this somewhere quiet." He kept talking as he walked, his voice increasing and decreasing with each breath as he moved. "Are you injured? Shit, Brady said your last game was brutal, but I haven't watched it yet."

"I'm not injured," Ten started, and then stopped. "Can I talk yet?"

There was the sound of a shutting door. "Okay, I'm in the video room."

"I'm gay, Jamie," Ten said confidently, and I squeezed his hand.

"Oh," Jamie said after a slight pause. "Okay."

"Do you have any questions?" Ten asked as it went quiet. "Should we talk?"

"About what?" Jamie asked. "I'm not talking to you about sex."

"Asshole, I meant about me."

"Nope."

Ten looked at me and shrugged. Even Brady looked confused.

"You're not angry?" Ten asked tentatively.

"Angry about what?"

"About me not telling you?"

"No," Jamie said immediately. "Why? Should I be?"

"Brady was."

Another pause. "You told Brady?" Jamie asked. "What did he say? Don't let him shout at you, Ten. He's an arrogant, pushy asshole who'll try to tell you what to do, but under it all he'll be worried. He's just crap at showing affection."

Brady huffed. "I'm here, actually," he announced.

Jamie didn't even react to that. "I knew you would be," he said. "Look, Ten, I don't care who you fall in love with. I'm your brother and I want you to be happy. Am I pissed you haven't told me? No. You must have had your reasons."

"I was going to tell you next week when we were in Florida."

Ten sounded so happy that Jamie was supportive, that Brady wasn't beating me up again. Weird how sentiment hits you when you know someone really well and all you want is for them to be happy all the time. That was how I felt about Ten. That was what love was like, I guessed.

"So why did you move it up to today? Because Brady is there? You have a matinee game with Boston, right?"

Ten blew out a soft breath, and I went from squeezing

his hand to lacing our fingers. I didn't know if he wanted that reassurance, but I certainly needed it.

"Brady walked in on me and my boyfriend." He looked at me as he said that.

"Okay, so you have a boyfriend. Cool."

"I've had to tell management, and my agent, and the team is next after you and Brady."

"Wait, did you tell Mom and Dad yet?"

"Yep, they've booked all three of their sons into the next Pride parade."

"Cool," Jamie said. "I'm up for that. Wait again, who are you involved with?" He lowered his voice to a whisper. "Is it another player?"

"It's Mads."

"Jeez, I thought you just said Mads."

"I did."

"Jared Madsen? That Mads?"

"Yeah."

There was a very definite and prolonged sigh at Jamie's end. "He's a good guy," he finally offered. "Tell him if he hurts you I'll kill him."

I tapped a finger on the counter to indicate that I wanted to talk. "Jamie, Mads here. I promise you, if I ever hurt Ten, you can take it in turns killing me."

Silence. Why was there silence? I was feeling fidgety when the line remained quiet. Jamie was like that—the peace-maker, the thinker, the one who had these weird periods of quiet when he said very little in the way of anything at all.

"I love him," I said to fill that space, and then, because it was as vital to me as my next breath, I unlaced our fingers and cradled Ten's face. "I love you," I said as I stared into his beautiful eyes. "I'm too old for you, I have a kid, and I have Ev on my back all the time. I don't rake in the big bucks anymore, but I do cook a mean omelet, and I love you, Ten."

Weird that my first declaration of love was with witnesses. Somehow it was important that I say it at that moment. As if saying it in front of his brothers would show Ten it was real. I hoped Ten didn't think I'd cheapened the whole thing.

He didn't. He rubbed a cheek against my hand, the silk of his hair on my fingers. "I love that you're older than me, and I love omelets," he said, "as long as there's no mushrooms. And I love you too."

Nah, he clearly didn't think it was cheap or wrong for us to be doing this in front of his brothers.

No, it was actually Brady and Jamie who ruined the moment, making simultaneous gagging noises and then teasing Ten.

Leaving the three of them to talk was all kinds of easy. They had things to say to each other, and I went to my bedroom. This was my space. Personal photos, dark bedding, a gorgeous view over the lake from one window and the front gardens from the other. The ceiling was tall, the bed huge, and there was plenty of room for two hockey players to stay in there.

So, I guessed this wasn't my room anymore. And with that in mind, wanting Ten to be with me when I woke in the morning and when I went to bed at night, I began clearing out one side of the closet to make room for his stuff. This was a statement I was making—giving him space, making this permanent.

I could imagine his smile when he saw what I'd done made my heart expand in my chest. I was a sappy, mushy idiot over Ten, and I didn't care who knew it. Or, at least who in the family knew it. I wasn't ready to be the one to expose Ten to the entire world, and we'd cross that bridge when we came to it.

"Breakfast," Ten said from behind me, pushing his hands down past the waistband of my sweats. "I love you."

I turned awkwardly, kissed him, and he hugged me so hard I couldn't breathe at first; he had one hell of a grip.

"You know I need to tell the team," he said as I held him close.

He was right; the Railers were a good bunch of guys, a family. I was convinced they would support him, and if they didn't, I'd *educate* them. With my words, of course. Not my fists.

I'm not a Neanderthal.

TWELVE

Tennant

B reakfast with Brady. Wow, it was something special. I mean, being able to sit with my older brother—who was generally a massive bag of dicks—by Mads' side and talk freely about shit had been an amazing experience. While he still had that elitist attitude about hockey and the Railers, he seemed to have found some respect for me as a man. Everything in my life was clicking into place. Sure, there were things that we needed to work through. Like being out with Mads but not really being *out* with Mads, if that makes sense. We went places, but were careful not to touch in an intimate way or show any signs of being anything other than friends or player/coach. It kind of sucked. No, it *really* sucked. I began wondering if coming out to the world might be the way to go. Then, at least, we'd be able to hold hands at the movies and not have to sneak into each other's homes. Homes. That was another thing that needed to be thought about.

But for now I had to concentrate on afternoon hockey against my big brother's team.

This was what it was all about. The crowds chanting my name, the smell of men in sweaty pads, the spray of ice, the sound of bodies and pucks bouncing off the boards, the knowledge that you just stole the puck from your older brother and got a quality scoring chance. Heh, yeah. Hockey.

"You're making Brady look like a minor-leaguer," Addison said during a line change.

I bumped gloved knuckles with him. Yeah, Brady was working hard to keep me covered. It was the match-up of the day. The press had been slobbering over Rowe vs. Rowe for days now, playing up the "youth and speed vs. age and experience" angle. The truth was that the second line—which was still my line, damn it to fucking hell—was outmatching Boston every time we were on the ice. But that outmatching came at a cost. Boston was a big, physical team. Always had been and always would be. They played with an edge. I had no doubt that when I was next out on the ice, Brady would make me pay for stealing that puck so easily from his stick.

We were rolling into the bottom of the second period with two fat goose eggs on the scoreboard. The Railers were keeping up well with the big, bad boys from Boston, though. We had the edge in face-off wins, but Boston was creaming us with blocked shots and hits. Like, their hits tally must be in the hundreds by now, or maybe it just felt that way. Brady had driven my ass into the boards so many times I'd lost count. I'd be a huge walking bruise tomorrow.

I spat my mouth guard into my hand, rinsed my mouth with water, spat that onto the floor between my skates, then grabbed my other bottle and downed some Gatorade. Seven minutes left in the period. After I rehydrated, a trainer tossed me a clean towel. I scrubbed my face and then my visor, feeling the hum of the game in my marrow.

Mads was instructing, aka yelling at the defense. He wanted more net-front pressure on the Boston goalie. That would be nice. So, then the next play, one of the Railers puts lots of pressure on the goalie. So much that he ends up in the penalty box with a two-minute goaltender interference call. Dumbass.

I shoved my mouth guard back in and threw my legs over the boards. I was always out for first shift of the penalty kill. And of course, when one Rowe boy was on the ice, here came the other.

"Would you stop following me around? Shit, little brothers are so fucking annoying," Brady chirped as he skated past in all his "I'm the Captain, just look at my big C" glory.

The other Boston players thought that was funny. I kind of did too, but I'd never let him know it.

"I'm just staying behind to catch you in case you totter and fall over, old man."

The Railers found great humor in my reply. I saw a spark of amusement in Brady's dark eyes. I slipped into position for the face-off. The Boston center mumbled something about my mother that made me a little mad. I snapped the puck from under his big nose and fired it to a winger. That Boston center and I stayed at the dot talking to each other after the play headed down into our zone.

"You know you just called your team captain's mother a dirty snatch, right?"

"No, I was calling *your* mother… Fuck. You suck dick, then. How about that, fucking pretty boy?"

I took a swing, because that was my mother he was talking about. Gloves hit the ice—his first, I need to point out. There was no way I was coming out on top of this fight, but I gave it my best. I managed to land a blow to his shoulder. He got a jab to my right eye in before we fell to the ice, pulling on sweaters and pummeling shoulder pads. Whistles were blowing steadily now. We were pulled apart and led to our respective penalty boxes, chirping all the while. I flopped down beside Arvy. He thumped me on the shoulder with the side of his fist.

"Good on you, kid," Arvy crowed.

My brother skated over to the Railers box to hand me my gloves and stick. "You know we're going to score now, right? That was stupid." He shoved my gear at me, then skated off.

Yeah, he was right. It had been stupid to remove myself from the PK and leave us down two men, but it felt good to wrestle that asshole down to the ice. My mother was not a dirty snatch, although I *did* suck dick. *Guess he was half right.* And Brady was right about them scoring, the fuckers. Arvy and I both got our asses chewed when we were back in the dressing room between periods.

Third period seemed to get even more physical. Brady had gulped down some magic elixir or something, because I could not shake him when I was on the ice. He was all over me, pushing, pushing, pushing, until he pushed just a little too hard. I had the puck about ten minutes into the third period and was racing at the Boston net. Brady knew there was no way he could catch me flat out, so he had only one choice to pull me off my direct intercept course, and that was to grab my arm and hold it. Off he went for a two-minute sit in the sin bin. Now, finally, with a man advantage, maybe we could tie this puppy up.

There was lots of chatter on ice before the faceoff. I'd been pulled off to rest and prepare for the second shift of the power play. The first unit hit the Boston net hard, firing shot after shot, but all of them into the chest of the goalie. When I was on the ice, I decided that I was going to stop trying to elevate the puck on each shot. The Boston tendie was not going to let anything go high. Going low would be the only way to sneak one past him. Hopefully we could get lots of dusky blue sweaters in the crease to block his sharp eyes. We got our chance with fifty seconds left of the power play. After Boston had iced the puck, we were facing off in the defensive zone of the offending team, which in this case was Boston. My wingers were spaced out nicely and the two D-men were tight. Me and Big Nose smiled at each other.

"Nice eye. You ain't so pretty now," he mumbled as the puck dropped through the air.

I dug in, got the puck, and shuttled it to Arvy. He passed it to Addison, who took a weak shot that the Boston goalie deflected into the air. The puck came down behind the net. I shook off Big Nose with a quick move that sent him skating past me, his stick dangerously close to a hook around my middle. There was a pile-up over the puck, players lunging at it like a pack of hungry dogs. Sticks clattered, men growled, and the puck shot out of the assembly behind the Boston net and bounced off the corner board. Our ice is weird. I knew that the puck would come off that curved board and take a funky hop. It always did. Being the home team has its advantages.

I pushed out of the knot of men on skates, raced to the point I knew the puck would reach, and picked it up after that wonky bounce took place. I drew back and hit the puck with all I had. The slap shot bounced like a tennis ball, the puck juking up into the air then coming down right in front of the Boston tender. It rolled between his legs on its side and into the net. The red light behind the Boston goal came on. The horn sounded, and I threw myself against the glass, beating on it as the Railers fans on the other side did the same.

The other men on the ice swarmed over me, patting my helmet and congratulating me. Skating down the line to rap knuckles with all the players, I looked at the coaches. Mads gave me a smile and a nod. Benning seemed delighted. Then I tapped my helmet with my fingers at the Rowe brother who had just exited the penalty box. Brady just shook his head, then went to sit down.

No one else scored after that. The goalies had locked shit down. We pushed through a five-minute overtime and still no goals. The shootout would have to determine the winner. Getting one point for the tie was okay, but we *needed* that other point. Our division was killer tight already, and every point was going to be critical. Also, beating Brady was just a thing that had to happen.

Coach sent me out first to face off against the Boston goalie. He tapped the pipes as I skated out to center ice, kind of like a "Bring it, punk" gesture. Arrogant SOB. Turned out he had a right to be arrogant. I tried my best, pulling a trick out of my hat that I'd seen one of the Rangers wingers do once. It was a slow approach to the net with a quick wrist snap to send the puck past the tender. Seemed like that Rangers forward had that move locked down, because my shot went right into the Boston goalie's big catching glove.

The bench was vocal when it was our turn again. Our captain snuck one in with a glorious little toe-drag move and a deke. After that it was the Stan Show. That massive Russian in our net turned into a brick wall. When the final shooter for Boston—my brother—failed to sneak a shot past Stan, we all went to our skates with hoots and shouts. Then we went out to hug the towering Russian, who was smiling broadly, the big chump.

Stan was chosen as the first star of the game, and rightfully so. He'd faced forty-two shots and only allowed one in. I got second star for my goal. It was a great game. The dressing room was wild pumped. I sat in my cubicle grinning, my gaze roaming over the gathered men. My team. It was time the men I played with knew they had a gay man in the ranks. But telling them there felt wrong. I didn't want to bring down the emotions with what might be a badly received announcement. Maybe over food? Mom always baked Dad treats when she had something bad to tell him, like that time she'd backed into a tree with the new car. He'd come home to find a triple-layer white coconut cake waiting for him.

"Hey, dinner's on me!" I shouted so that I was heard over the din. "And yes, that means I'm paying," I added when no one responded.

Soon as they knew I was footing the bill, the team cheered. What a bunch of A-holes. We all agreed to meet at this cool little sports bar/eatery right off the Capital Beltway.

I found Mads in his office after the game. "Hey," I called after rapping on the open door.

He glanced up from his laptop, and his smile almost knocked me out of my shoes. Have I mentioned how lush the man is?

"I'm taking the team over to Roger's by the Beltway for dinner to celebrate. You coming?"

"I have videos to make for the game against Pittsburgh."

"Oh man, that sucks." I leaned a hip against the doorframe. "See you later, then?" Which was secret, gay-player-having-a-relationship-with-his-coach code for, "I'll see you at your place. I love you and I plan to suck your dick as a private celebration."

"Yep," Mads said as his gaze lingered on my mouth. "Oh. Nice eye." Yeah, he was so getting his dick sucked as soon as I got home.

I jogged off to meet up with Stan and Addison. The Boston team was leaving. We met in the corridor. Brady dropped an arm around my shoulders.

"You guys got lucky this time," he announced loudly while tugging me into his side a time or two.

"Yeah, right. You're just all butt hurt over being whipped by an expansion team," I countered. He tightened his arm playfully around my throat, then shoved me away.

"No one likes a wise-ass," he said as we walked outside. Early November was damn cold in Pennsylvania. I didn't like it. "You coming home for Thanksgiving?"

"Oh, uh, man, I really don't know. Depends." More secret code that meant I didn't know what Mads was doing for turkey day, Mom and Dad didn't know about Mads, and I wasn't sure even where I'd be living by the end of the month. "I'll see and let them know.

"No, none of that shit. You get your ass home. It'll be cool."

"Thanks," I said as sincerely as I could. "Thanks for the two points."

"Brat," he chuckled.

He shook my hand, then hustled into the waiting charter bus that would take them to the airport and back to Boston. After waving, I hurried to my Jeep, got inside, cranked it over and turned the heat to the broil setting. Jesus. It must be forty degrees out there. Winter in the north was going to be tough for this beach baby.

Arriving at Roger's Ribs got me a rousing round of cheers from the patrons of the sports bar and restaurant.

Fans left their seats and meals to come talk to me, take selfies, or have me sign something.

"Man, Rowe, all the ladies do love you!" Arvy shouted when I finally wiggled free from the knot of females giggling and batting their lashes. "What's your secret?"

I shrugged and sat down next to Connor. My captain inclined his head, then led the team into some long-winded tale about when he was playing in the minors up in Saskatoon. It was a cool move, although I was used to deflecting chick comments. Food started arriving then, as well as pitchers of soda. Steaks and pork chops, whole roasted chickens, platters of pasta of every shape and size. We dove in, eating and joking, telling our own stories and reliving beating Boston a few dozen times. The food disappeared quickly. Twenty hungry hockey players can really put grub away. Amid all the laughter and dirty jokes, I could feel us bonding. The servers were kept hopping, but were friendly and cute, flirting a bit with the guys as they cleared off the dinner plates and brought out desserts and coffee. I sipped some coffee and watched the guys interacting. Then I leaned to the side and whispered to Arvy.

"Hey, I'm gay. Pass it around the table."

He drew back and looked at me as if I'd just said I was Queen Victoria. "Really?"

"Truth, man." I smiled, and then jerked my chin at the team to make him get whispering.

We used to play that game all the time when I was a kid. Each man got the whisper, looked at me, then passed it on. By the time it had traveled around the table and landed in Stan's ear, I was chuckling. The big goalie stared at me openly, scratched his long nose, and then asked the table, "Tennant Queen of May? What is mean?"

We all lost it, and we all stayed *way* later than we

should've. I crept into Mads' place around two. He was sound asleep, long arms and legs taking up most of the bed. I stripped and wiggled under the covers, seeking his body out in the dark. He barely stirred when I pressed my cold ass tight to his side. He did make a kind of purring sound of contentment, but then returned to softly snoring. I dropped off quickly now that I was warm and next to Mads.

When I woke up, I rolled around, groggy and confused, trying to figure out what had woken me. It hadn't been Mads, because he wasn't even in the bed. I flopped onto my back and yawned, then heard him talking. Okay, so maybe it had been Mads. And talking wasn't the right term. He was pushing words through gritted teeth. Seething. Snarling. Whoever had called had the man fired up. I rolled my head and saw that it was five minutes after six. For the sake of all fucks, who was calling this early and giving Jared shit? I kicked off the covers and stumbled out into the living room, rubbing my eye while scratching the dry skin on my stomach. Heat and winter. It was making me itch. Ugh. I needed Southern heat and humidity, stat.

"Dude, what's the issue? It's not even seven yet," I said, and got a look from my boyfriend. Was it cool to call him that? And was it cool to be eye-stabbed at asshole o' clock in the morning by the dude you planned to suck off? No. No, it was not.

"Ten, please," Mads snapped. "Ev, we've been over this before. He's doing this my way."

Mads' glower was still resting on me. I gave him the middle finger, then fell face-first onto the couch.

"It's no one. Look, who I have in my home is my business. Just as Ryker is. Yes, that's my final word. Now drop this or I'm going to… Ev? You fuck, did you hang up on me?"

Face buried in the cushion, I heard the crunchy sound

of cell phone meeting wall. I pushed myself onto my right side. Mads was standing in front of me looking like he was one blink from a full-on meltdown.

"You want a blowjob?" I asked.

Let's face it, oral sex makes everything better. And he was naked and his dick was particularly tempting and I was kind of horny. Mads lowered his gaze from the phone-and-wall massacre to me. I gave him a quick waggle of an eyebrow. A creaky sort of smile appeared.

"I'm totally serious," I said. "Blowjobs are the best."

"Sex doesn't solve every problem, Tennant."

"So, are you saying you don't want me to suck you off?"

"I'm saying that sex won't make Ev less of a controlling… what's that term you always use?"

"Dick sock?"

That one made him snort. "Okay, not that one, but it works."

"Yep. So, about that blowjob…"

He sat down next to me, pulled me onto his lap, and just held me, his head cradled on my shoulder. He talked as he held me. Told me every damn sick thing that Ev—the cockmonkey—had ever done to him, his son, and Ryker's mom.

"You okay?" I asked after several minutes passed with him stroking the tat on the back of my neck.

"I will be after a little more touching."

"You want me to touch your dick?"

His big body shook with laughter. "My God, you're single-minded. That will take you far in life."

"Will it take me to your bedroom?" I wiggled around, bare ass rubbing on naked thighs.

"No, but it will take you a little deeper into my heart."

He was lying. It did take me into his bedroom after just

RJ SCOTT & V.L. LOCEY

a little more wiggling. Never give up. Rules any coach and player should live by.

———

"IS THERE a reason you're standing there staring at the closet?" Mads called as we were getting ready for bed that night.

I turned to look at him. "You made room for me."

He nodded, and then went back to unbuttoning his dress shirt. I'd peeled my suit off as soon as we'd walked in and was now skipping around in just my briefs. Mads didn't seem to mind.

"Are we sure this is what we want?" I asked.

"'We' as in 'us' or 'we' as in 'me'?" He tossed the dirty shirt into the hamper.

"'We' as in 'you,' because I'm not sure if you get what that gesture means." I waved a hand at the closet behind me.

"Tennant, I am fully aware of what making room for your clothes means." A smile played on his lips. The man was *so* fucking lush, even with the shiner blooming. Fucking stupid Brady.

"If I do this, that means I'm going to have to come out. Like, there is no way we can live together with me not being out."

"People do it all the time." He picked my pants up from the end of the bed and chucked them in his hamper.

All this was getting overwhelming. Closet space, moving in, his clothes getting friendly with mine in his hamper, maybe coming out.

"Yeah, but we're not 'people.'" I tossed some air quotes up. "I'm Tennant Rowe. You're Jared Madsen. We're involved in professional sports. We have cameras in our faces all the time, Mads."

"And that scares you."

"I don't know. Maybe a little, yeah." I pushed my fingers through my hair. "I never wanted to be the gay hockey poster boy, Mads. I just want to play hockey and love who I love."

"That would be me."

"Yes, you massive dork, that would be you."

He winked. I chuckled. The pressure eased off just a bit.

"Now I'm totally wound up because the thought of moving in here with you makes me feel like I just ate a live squid."

"And that's a good feeling, I assume?" He tugged his belt free from the loops of his pants, rolled it neatly and placed it into a dresser drawer. Mine was lying on the floor by the foot of the bed.

"Well, mostly, yeah," I said, and then padded over to pick up my belt. I handed it to him. He nodded, then rolled it up and laid it beside his. I found myself staring at our two belts coiled up in that drawer. "I really want to move in here with you. Bring my PlayStation and my piano and just be with you, but…"

"But the world." He ran his hand over my biceps, pulling my attention off belts snuggling together. "Tennant, I'm not going to rush you." His eyes were so brilliant and warm. Like a spring sky or a robin's egg. "The space is yours *whenever* you decide to make use of it. I know you can't just run home and grab your piano tonight."

"Right, because that old bitch is heavy and will *not* fit into any duffel bag I own," I pointed out. My gaze moved to the mirror attached to the dresser. I saw Mads and me standing side by side in the looking glass. "What should I do?" I asked the blond man in the mirror.

"You do what feels right when it feels right," he told my reflection.

"That's no help at all."

"It's the best I can do. Let's go to bed, Tennant. I'm tired and we have a game tomorrow."

"Yeah, right." I closed the belt drawer but left the closet open.

THIRTEEN

Mads

The hit wasn't hard. It wasn't even a full check, more a collection of bodies in and around the net, but it couldn't have come at a worse time.

One-zero in our favor, and the puck bouncing on some of the shittiest ice I'd seen all season. I'd switched up my first D-pair, got them on the ice in a smooth changeover, and I took a moment just to admire the play evolve. I could feel the goal, like sometimes you just know the puck is going to pass the minder and find the net. Their goalie had been a beast tonight, and there was frustration in our team to break him. But with only five minutes left in the game, it seemed he wasn't about to start letting shots through now.

But we had the puck. Mac passed to Arvy from behind our goal, Arvy cycled it back, got in position, waited for the next changeover, first line was right there on the ice, and then it was game on. Two quick tape-to-tapes, a beautiful saucer from Lee, and Connor Hurleigh had the puck, steadying the bounce, heads up, and then he just let that beauty fly. Their defense bundled into Connor, the goalie went down, reached for the puck but it was too damn quick, hundred miles an hour, and the Railers were two up.

The boos and jeers from the away crowd were something to ignore, the cheers from the Railers fans behind our bench and the shouts of the team outweighing anything from the home team supporters. The other team's defense were still hovering at the goal mouth, some kind of altercation between our first line and them, and then everyone moved away and revealed Connor, our captain, hunched over and clearly in pain.

"What the fuck?" Coach shouted, and even as he said that our medics were up and over the boards and straight to him. Linesmen congregated, and a weird hush fell over the crowd. I couldn't properly see from where I was, and I exchanged glances with Ten, who was leaning over the boards and staring down at the ice.

How badly was Connor hurt? Was his year over? Was it a broken bone, or a knee out of joint, a torn ACL, or even worse, that ghost of hell; a concussion. I only realized I was clutching my chest when Coach tapped me on the shoulder.

"Okay?" he asked, and pointed at the fist right over my heart.

I dropped it immediately, but not before Ten had caught the same action. He didn't know where to look—at his captain clambering up with help from medics, or his lover probably looking like he was about to keel over dead.

"Yeah," I said, and then desperately wanted to change the narrative of the whole situation here. No one mentioned my medical issues anymore—not the team, not my friends, not even my son. They were filed under 'things his body and hockey did to him'.

Of course, I was still introduced as Jared Madsen, "former Sabres defender. Retired after a hit in the Stanley

Cup final—heart problems, you know" by anyone who wanted to make it clear why I wasn't still playing. I didn't need anyone to defend me or explain the reasons why I'd stopped playing. Equally, I didn't want to see that expression on Ten's face. He'd looked like someone had kicked his puppy.

"What's the news?" I asked Emma, our first medic, as she skated back over. She shook her head; we weren't exactly going to share medical information about a player with any asshole who could lip-read. But her expression was serious, and Cole, our second medic, had to hold Connor upright with help from Arvy.

This did not look good, and the pain on Connor's face was something I hated to see on any player.

"Heads back in the game," Coach shouted.

The entire team looked at him before he sent over the second line but kept Ten back and sent out our third line center. This was mixing up the lines to try to keep momentum, and Ten stared intently at the game. When he went over alongside the first line wingers, centering his own first line, my heart was in my mouth. Their D was all over our forwards, and this move put him up against the same big boys that had just taken out our captain.

It wasn't a disaster, not like the *Titanic* was a disaster, but more of an experiment that didn't entirely work. Ten hadn't played with these two guys. He was faster than them; that much was obvious. With his own line, he'd learned how to use that speed. With these two guys, he was all over the show and asking too much for his wingers to connect, and these were the best we had.

The three of them were just puzzle pieces that didn't quite fit. Two minutes left and the other team scored on us. One minute left and it was tied when Ten turned over the puck in the neutral zone. The game ended in a tie, moving the whole thing into overtime. The three-on-three was just as brutal. Somehow, none of the team out there were connecting with anyone, like Connor being injured had ripped the structure of the team to shreds for this game and we'd lost all composure. Even Coach wasn't cursing as he normally did. Connor being hurt was big. A game changer.

When our opponents scored at three twenty-seven into the five-minute overtime, the fans erupted, and we left the bench, going straight to the dressing room. Players first. Inconsolable players who all wanted to know one thing. *How is Connor? Is Connor okay? Is he playing the next game?*

This was dangerous. This could derail everything.

"We don't know anything," Coach explained to the very quiet room. "It's nine thirty. I want us on the coach at ten thirty, okay? Flying at eleven."

Everyone nodded, and I saw Ten slump in his stall, hands between his knees, his head bowed. I wanted to tell him it was okay, that having an injured captain wasn't the end of the world, that we would rally, he could step up, we could win the following ten games in a row.

If only I felt that optimism inside. Ten was exposed out there, and I couldn't see it changing by the next game.

THE PLANE WAS QUIET. Connor had limped onto it without help. The injury wasn't career ending, but nobody on the medical team was telling us anything. All they would say is it would be a while for assessment, possibly missing two weeks of games. I thought about who we were facing. Six games over the next two weeks—a stand of four in a row at home, the other two in Florida.

Ten used the bathroom, walking past me, his hand

brushing my shoulder, and God how I wanted, at that moment, to push him into the bathroom and just…

Hold him.

All I wanted to do was tell him all those things to reassure him. And how stupid was that? When he walked back, he still had that destroyed expression on his face, and I stopped him with a hand on his thigh.

"You played well. Get over the loss and move on," I said. As a coach, I could say those kinds of things, and no one would bat an eyelid.

Ten simply looked at me and nodded. "Yes, Coach," he murmured, and I let him go.

We were back in Harrisburg by two, taking separate cars home, always careful, and by the time I'd finished talking to Coach, the players' cars were gone and I knew Ten would be home.

He was in bed when I got in, and I stripped, brushed my teeth, and curled up behind him in bed.

"How serious is it?" Ten asked.

"They're saying groin strain. Could've been worse; he could've impacted the wall."

Ten snuggled back into my hold, and it took a while, but finally he slept.

THE NEXT DAY AT THE COACHES' meeting, they composed the official statement of a lower body injury, and then it was all about who to move where. A huge amount of what they were saying was focused on Ten.

Coach seemed to change his mind with each separate input from his coaches.

Ten was strong. Ten was fast. Ten was *too* strong. Ten was *too* fast.

I thought they were missing one vital thing, and when it was my turn to talk I had to push down the instinct that maybe my opinion was tainted by the fact I loved Ten.

I loved hockey—the purity of it, the grace and beauty and style—and I had always stayed honest to the game as a player and a coach. So, I had to trust that what I wanted to say was purely technical and didn't focus on Ten's determination, and his huge heart that meant he'd sacrifice everything for this team.

"I agree," I began carefully. "Ten is way too fast for the wingers from our existing first line, but I honestly think we shouldn't throw the line under the bus. We need to get Ten to adjust, but to my mind he's first line for sure."

"I'll work with the three of them," Coach said, and nodded to Pikey, the associate coach. "Let's get them in."

WE LOST THE NEXT GAME, not because of one line in particular, but because the team as a whole was all over the damn place. I was hoarse with shouting and dizzy with trying to match the lines. We were lucky to get away with only a five-two loss. It wasn't what the team needed; it wasn't what Ten needed. He overcompensated and lost any kind of natural edge he had to his skating. He was frustrated, the team was disappointed… we needed to pull this back, all of us.

We won the next game, after a combination of the team being fresh off a back-to-back and starting their backup goalie. It wasn't a pretty win, messy and scrappy, but it was a win. Another win in Nashville, and I caught Ten's brief almost-smile, and it was in that game that I saw something click out there. Ten was different. He was talking with authority in the room, he was guiding and working on plays, and he was stepping up to his first line responsibilities.

Well, at the rink he was. On TV he was.

At home? That was a different matter. Everything flooded out on the day off after our latest win. We'd woken up, made love as usual, eaten breakfast like every other day, drunk coffee, talked shit… we'd even shared a shower and some pretty freaking awesome kissing.

But when it came to deciding what to do with our day, a toss-up between going out for lunch or staying in and watching cheesy movies that we could ridicule, Ten was clearly agitated. He couldn't decide; he wouldn't decide. He had no opinion on what we should do, and he began to pace. I contemplated going out for a walk, giving him some space to let him get everything out of his system on his own, but it seemed he wanted to talk.

"I'm not ready for the first line on this team," he announced on his twenty-something pass of the sofa in front of me.

Ah. So that was what was up.

"Yes, you are," I said, and I believed it. I wouldn't lie because, like I said, you have to be honest in hockey. I'd never blown smoke up any player's ass; I wasn't going to start now. Ten had to know I was being candid, right? Only his next words showed he thought very little about what I was saying at all.

"You're just saying that because we're together."

"My dick up your ass doesn't mean I'm lying," I said crudely, and saw him wince.

That had been harsh, and I realized I needed to lose my coach persona and really find my inner kindness. It came out wrong, because what I wanted to say was, *Talk to me, Ten. Let's see if we can't sort this, and I'll be super supportive and boyfriend-y.* But what actually came out was, "Fuck's sake, Ten, don't be so hard on yourself."

Yep, even after all of the your-heart-is-for-shit, hockey-is-done therapy, on occasion I was still a dick who couldn't word things the right way.

Ten sat on the coffee table in front of me, his knees bumping mine. "I wanted that first line so bad," he admitted. "But not at Connor's expense."

"So, what is it? You feel guilty that Connor was injured and you took his spot?"

"Yes, no… yes… Shit, I don't know."

Ten looked adorably confused, and I leaned forward and placed my hands on his knees. "That's hockey, Ten. You know that."

He looked at me and nodded, but the worry hadn't left his expression. "So, what if I'm better centering the second line?"

"You might be," I said, then made sure to add the reassurance part. "But the coaches and management see a strong improvement from you on that first line, and you'll be stronger on second when Connor is back."

He nodded. "I wanted that first line," he admitted in a soft voice, like he was admitting the world's worst sin. "But I wanted to earn it. And how stupid is that? Because the game we play means we could all get injured tomorrow."

"Exactly. Play your position, play your best. Part of the team."

"All those years being second best behind Tate Collins, I wanted to show I was the best, but maybe I'm better off in second place."

"That's bullshit and you know it," I said, and there must have been something in my tone, because Ten smiled at me, a heart-stopping smile that reached his beautiful eyes. I was a goner. I tugged him so he was next to me on the sofa, then pulled him close. "And one day," I teased, "when you're a grown-up boy, you can be captain of your own team."

That was enough for him to start a play fight, which in turn led to kissing, which of course inevitably led to some of the hottest sex I'd experienced in my entire life.

He is a drug and I am an addict.

———

THANKSGIVING ISN'T my favorite time of the year. I mean, Canadian Thanksgiving I love, but American Thanksgiving isn't a Canadian thing. Didn't matter, though, because suddenly, even though half our team was non-American, it was vital to know exactly how you were going to spend the day. Even Stan was into it, although how much he actually knew about Thanksgiving escaped me. When I asked him, all he said was "Eat ham. Gobble Gobble".

Seemed to me that where each of us was spending that one day was all anyone could talk about, and I'd been personally invited to four separate turkey days as the sad loner the team saw me as. I didn't even explain I'd have Ryker with me because his mom and her husband were on a tenth-anniversary cruise.

All I can say is thank fuck for Ten.

"Hey, Coach, Brady said you should go visit him for Thanksgiving." Ten said, loud enough that anyone who was bothering to hang around talking post-game would hear. Subtle was not in Ten's vocabulary.

"He did?"

"Yep. Him and Jamie will be at Mom and Dad's, and I'm going as well. You wanna go?"

"I have Ryker," I said, picking up my bag. I'd already

planned for the worst-case scenario of some Ten-free days, but when Casey had told me about her last-minute thing, I'd been happy to get to enjoy the day off with Ryker. Star Wars movies and a huge amount of over-eating on anything but turkey were in the plans. Ten had walked in on the conversation last week, so he'd known I had Ryker, but neither of us had made anything like a plan.

"Yeah, Mom said Ryker should come too."

Which was how we'd got to the place where we were now. Sitting on a bench and lacing up skates at the Railers practice rink. We weren't in Carolina yet. This was the prequel to the Thanksgiving fun; Ryker had come up early, and he'd talked non-stop about going skating with me and Ten. The facility was closed, it was eleven at night, the lights were low, it was just the three of us, and I was going out on the ice for the first time with Ten.

Well, not the first time, but the first without my coach's hat, and maybe the chance of some two-on-one keep-away. I still had moves. My heart might have let me down, but muscle memory and the joy of skating were right there, front and center.

Ten and Ryker were chatting faster than I would have thought humanly possible, but every so often I saw Ten's eyes glaze over. Keeping up with my seventeen-year-old son was clearly wearing.

Then we were on the ice, and I watched with no small amount of pride as Ryker pushed with his foot and found a skating rhythm that was fast and accurate, finishing the push with some backward crossovers and lazy circles around me and Ten. Ryker pushed off again, taking a puck with him and warming up with a few slow passes to himself off the boards.

"He's good, and I'm not just saying that as his dad," I

said. "He's better than his age dictates; Ev already wants him tied up to an agent."

Ten glanced at me, then back to Ryker. "No," he said. "Not after what happened to Brady, remember?"

I remembered all too well; the scumbag who'd screwed Brady over had made it difficult for him to get away from the minors and almost fucked up his chances in the draft we shared.

"Ev will start in on me again. He's visiting."

"He's here?" Ten looked around, horrified, and I had to laugh. Ev and Ten hadn't exactly spoken other than a handshake on meeting, but Ten had certainly heard all the horror stories I'd told him.

"Tomorrow. Something about local business support, fuck if I know, but he has his finger in every pie that's remotely connected to me." I couldn't help the irritation in my voice, and it didn't stop. "And he's aware Ryker is with me for Thanksgiving, so I knew to expect his ass up in my space. Apparently, he wanted Ryker with him—something about me not being emotionally available, whatever the fuck that means."

Ryker came to a stop in front of us, throwing up snow. "Hey, old men, wanna skate?"

Ten straightened beside me and chuckled darkly, "You are so gonna pay for that, kid."

Ryker grinned like he'd expected nothing less and backed away from Ten, balancing a puck on the end of his stick. One knock from Ten and the puck landed on the ice, bouncing on its end, and Ten stole it from under him.

The two of them were a beautiful thing to watch. The two men in my life, laughing and teasing, then getting oh so serious. Ryker didn't stand a chance against Ten most of the time, but every so often—well, twice to be exact—coming up on Ten's left side, he would take the puck and he would make Ten work. I joined in, playing my lone defenseman role, stealing the puck, pretending to check Ryker into the boards. My breathing was fine, my heart was fine, but I couldn't keep up with Ryker, and there was no hope in hell of getting anywhere near Ten.

I'd come to terms with the age gap in my love life. Those extra years were nothing, and I loved Ten so much it hurt, so I forgot everything in that love, but in hockey terms, a decade was an eternity. Added to which, I wasn't as toned and fit as I used to be. I kept up pretty good, but I called time first. I skated to the boards and hoisted myself up, sitting there and watching Ryker and Ten dart around the ice.

My son had a future as a skater. One day he'd be that left wing people talked about. Hell, if Ten stayed healthy—And, why wouldn't he? After all, not everyone had a fucked-up heart like me—then Ryker might even play on Ten's wing.

It was possibly the best night of my life.

And from the way Ryker and Ten were currently rolling around on the ice with tears of laughter on their faces and Ryker giving Ten a snowy face-wash, I thought they might feel the same too.

THE GREAT JIMMY EVERETT, fabled left wing and star of the Red Wings back in the seventies, turned up halfway through morning practice, the last before our short Thanksgiving break. We were lucky this year—no game on turkey day, and the day off before and after. Win/win. Going to Ten's family's place was going to be a good use of the break, or so I kept telling myself.

But first I had to deal with Ev.

Coach called me over, inclining his head to where Ev stood talking to management. What the hell he was even doing this close to the Railers was open for debate. I'd seen him chatting to Ryker, but that didn't last long, with Ryker's body language screaming discomfort. Don't get me wrong, Ev was an okay grandpa as grandpas go, but he was also so focused on Ryker making the NHL at the earliest moment possible, and to the best team out there, that I think even Ryker was sick of it.

Ryker, in one of my Railers' hoodies, was next to Ev at that moment, and he looked like he was going to explode. Ev was chatting away to half the management team, who in turn fawned over him like he was freaking Gretzky or something.

I caught the end of some impressive backpedaling.

"What I mean by that," Ev was saying, with accompanying hand movements, "is that Ryker is certainly good enough for original six."

"Grandpa," Ryker hissed, scarlet with mortification.

"I see him back in Canada myself," he added. "So, I wasn't meaning to offend with my O6 comment."

"No offense taken," our marketing director lied. She exchanged looks with me—long-suffering and getting impatient type looks. "Anyway, please feel free to tour the rooms, and we'll meet back for lunch at one. Will that suit?"

Ev nodded. "I don't eat shellfish," he pointed out.

Abruptly, I pictured accidentally-on-purpose pushing Ev's head into a bucket of shrimp cocktail, and the image was so good I knew I would want to share it with Ten later.

"Ryker, you want to come with me?" I asked.

Ryker was at my side immediately, and I corralled him into the changing area, where I removed my skates. We shared the area with the team, the only demarcation between coaching staff and players a small wall at waist height. I loved this practice arena, just because I felt like I was inside the team, like there was no barrier.

Unfortunately, Ev followed us, looming over me.

"Patrick McNulty wants to talk to you. I gave him your number," he announced, his voice loud enough that everyone could hear. McNulty had a lot of the big guys, but I knew from experience that most of them wanted out.

"McNasty?" I began patiently. "The agent? The one whose blackmailing tape of that Leafs kid went viral?"

Ev huffed. "He's the best in the business, and I want him for Ryker."

"Fuck, no."

"Well I gave him your number." Ev crossed his arms over his chest like this was a done deal. "You'll talk to the man."

"No."

Ev turned to Ryker. "I'm trying my best for you, Ryker, but see what I have to put up with? Your *father* is like a brick wall here."

I slipped on my shoes—funny how I felt more settled knowing I had them on and could safely kick Ev's ass without breaking a toe—and stood up.

"For the last time, Ev. Ryker is too young for an agent. He is staying at school, he is finishing, he will join his eligible draft, and he will not burn out. At eighteen, his mother and I will go with him and interview as many goddamn agents as it takes to make sure he has the best representation, and it will be his decision."

Ev turned a funny shade of purple, and I could see the headlines now—Hockey Player Stands Up To Pseudo-Father-In-Law And Kills Him—but it wasn't a coronary, just a fit of temper, and fuck he'd been keeping it inside for a long time, because it hit me with the force of a tornado.

He leaned right into my space and he spat the words out like machine gun fire. "You think I don't see you pulling my grandson into your degenerate ways? You think I don't know about you and Rowe? Ryker stays with you, and I know for sure you and Rowe are probably fucking right in front of my grandson."

"Jesus, Grandpa," Ryker tried to interrupt, but Ev had a full head of steam and there was no stopping him.

"The moment you ruined my daughter I knew you were trash, and your deviancy is polluting everything that could be good about Ryker."

The words slid over me because they meant nothing, but the reaction in the room was very different.

The whole room, I mean.

The coaching staff and the entire Railers team were in this space, and Ev was losing his shit in front of an audience and outing the fact that Ten and I were together at the same time. Jesus Christ, this wasn't happening. I placed a calming hand on Ev's arm.

"Let's take this somewhere else."

"Mr. Everett, could we ask that you leave the area." This from Coach Benning, who moved closer.

Ev rounded on him and shook off my hand at the same time.

"Do you realize what kind of man you have working for you?" he asked Coach.

"A good man," was all Coach said. I could have kissed him.

His words didn't defuse the situation. Instead, Ev got louder. "He's sleeping with one of your skaters. You understand that, right? He's destroying your team like he's destroying Ryker's chances."

Then everything went to shit. Shit of unimaginable

proportions. Stan gripped Ev's upper arms and bodily lifted him away from me as Ryker slipped in between us.

"Make Hulk," The big goalie said, and deposited Ev behind him, blocking him. I looked at Ten, I looked at the team, then at the coaches.

"I can explain," I said. I'd take the blame, resign, tell everyone this was nothing, that Ten was a good guy and they shouldn't trade him or fucking lynch him or anything.

Ten ruined it all. He placed his hands on my shoulders and kissed me. Nothing too X-rated, just a soft kiss, then he backed away and turned to face the team. Some of the guys looked shocked. A couple were exchanging money. I only saw one really unhappy face, a new guy just traded in. Adler Lockhart, all mouth and attitude up in everyone's faces. He didn't seem happy at all.

"I'm in a committed relationship with Mads," Ten announced.

Ryker stood the other side of me, and I felt like the strongest and luckiest man on Earth.

"So yeah," I said a little late and with a whole lot of lame. "I'm with Ten."

Ev let out a snort of disgust. Stan simply picked him up in a fireman's carry and exited stage right. The coaching staff melted away, and Ryker went with them like he knew me and Ten needed to do this alone with the rest of the team.

"Guys?" Ten asked.

"Well, you sure like to make things hard for the team," Adler Lockhart laughed. "Can't we forget this happened? We don't need the stress of who checks out whose cocks in the dressing room."

"Fuck you Lockhart," Arvy snapped.

"Got no problem with you and coach being a thing," another voice said.

Even Adler finally murmured agreement after everyone stared at him.

Then Connor, who'd been watching practice from the bench and was now sat back in his stall, put two fingers in his mouth and whistled loudly.

"This doesn't leave the room," he said firmly.

I bristled. Hell, I could feel myself getting defensive.

"You want to talk to me alone?" Ten said from next to me, sounding more worried than I liked to hear. I clasped his hand; he wouldn't be doing that alone.

"No." Connor frowned. "Just, if you're keeping it on the down-low, you don't want the idiots in this room flapping their gums. We'll back you when you make it public. Okay?"

He wasn't asking us if that was okay, he was asking the team, and to a man they said yes.

Then he sighed noisily and hobbled over to us. "But seriously, guys, you might want to put a gag order on Everett."

I nodded. That was a given.

Now more people knew about our being in love.

And it was a good feeling.

FOURTEEN

Tennant

S tepping off the plane at Myrtle Beach International
Airport, I couldn't believe how cold it was. I burrowed
down into my Railers hoodie.

"Christ, it's freezing," I complained while Mads, Ryker,
and I disembarked. "It must be like fifty or something."

"Sissy beach boy," the Canadian behind me chuckled.

Giving him the bird as a reply was my first thought, but
since there were a couple old folks in front of me, I gave
him a dark look over my cold shoulder instead.

"Hell, we're out in tank tops and sandals when it hits
fifty in Ontario," Mads said.

"Good for you," I muttered.

Ryker chuckled at the banter. He was a really cool kid.
I know that some people would make all kinds of snide
comments about how close in age Ryker and I were when
Mads and I were public knowledge… *if* we were ever
public knowledge. Fuck the haters and everyone who
looked like them.

I hustled into the terminal to avoid frostbite. My folks
were right there, grinning madly. Mom got to me first,

pulling me into her arms and holding me tight for a long time. I embraced her tenderly, blinking at the moisture gathering in my eyes.

"My baby is home," she whispered by my ear. I gave my father an awkward smile as Mom clung to me like a Capuchin monkey.

"Okay Jean, we have to move. We're blocking traffic," Dad commented.

Mom pressed a kiss to my stubble-coated cheek. "*Now* it feels like Thanksgiving."

There was so much love in her eyes I had to cough and sniffle a bit before stepping away to motion to the men who'd flown down with me.

"This is Jared's son, Ryker."

"It's wonderful to meet you, Ryker."

Mom hugged him as well, but not as ferociously, and then pecked Mads on the cheek. Dad clapped Mads on the back, shook hands with Ryker, and then tugged me to his chest for a sound man-hug.

"It's good to have you home, Tennant," Dad told me as we headed to get our luggage.

After our bags were in hand, we hustled out to the parking lot. Mom herded us into their new red Dodge Durango. We all chatted during the drive from the airport to my parent's house.

We stepped out of the Durango and I glanced at Mads. He looked stressed, his mouth set and his eyes worried. I thought about taking him for a walk to the beach just a block away, but my mother was already pulling me toward the house.

Mads threw an arm around Ryker, whispering something into his son's ear. The roar that rolled out of the front door when Dad pulled it open made Ryker's eyes flare.

"Twin two-year-olds," I shouted over the high-pitched squeaky giggles that met us at the door.

Brady's girls were dressed alike in tan overalls over white lacy tops. Their dark hair was pulled into those little Pebbles Flintstone top-of-the-head ponytails. The girls saw Ryker and Mads, then ran off screaming at the top of their lungs.

"Mom, you seriously need to hand out ear plugs at the door."

Total bedlam erupted. Jamie raced past with one twin on his shoulders, Brady the other girl, both stopping only long enough to say "Yo" to me, Mads, and Ryker before thundering off.

"Welcome to the loony bin," Dad chuckled as children squealed and wives shouted at husbands to stop rough-housing in their parents' house. "It'll be like this until the boys leave," he tacked on, for Mads' sake, I think.

"It's as lively as I remember," Mads commented while peeling off his jacket.

Mom took our coats and hung them in the hall closet, then herded us into the madness. Kids, toys, two Lisa's, Brady's black lab, Bourque, and my brothers. We were shoved into the melee. It felt like home. Loud, rowdy, and slightly crazed. I introduced Mads and Ryker to Brady's and Jamie's wives. Blonde Lisa and Brunette Lisa, respectively.

"So, am I not going to fit in here, not being a Lisa?" Mads whispered to me as we lounged on the couch catching up. That made me laugh. I wanted to pat his thigh or lean in for a kiss, but I'd not quite found the right way to tell my parents about me and Mads. I would... hopefully.

Dinner was pizza and wings that night, since Mom said she had enough cooking the next day. By the time the pizza was gone, Mads had lost some of the tension lines around his mouth and eyes. We watched old Stephen Seagal movies until midnight. Sitting beside Mads all night, his hip and thigh next to mine, but not being able to touch him had driven me slightly crazy. I'd rolled a thousand scenarios about a secret tryst around in my head, but two things stood in the way. The fact that Mads was sleeping in the man cave with his son on the pullout sofa, and the idea of having sex in my parents' house. There was just something squicky about doing it where my mother might hear. Now doing it where she *couldn't* hear...

"Hey," I whispered to Mads after everyone had headed for their beds. "Meet me in the back yard in an hour."

His eyebrows knotted.

"Just do it."

I jogged up to my old bedroom and spent the next hour reading over some old comics from a box in my closet. When my phone alarm sounded softly, I grabbed a Railers hoodie from my bag, tugged it on, and slipped quietly past all the sleeping Rowes, then down the stairs, carefully avoiding the sixth step, which creaked loudly. Mads was standing in the kitchen in nothing but fleece pants and a tank top, his shoulders looking so much broader than his lean waist. Yeah, I needed me some of that.

"Come on," I whispered, then carefully unlocked the back door. Out I went into the night. "Fuck, it's cold."

"Tennant, what the hell is this all about?" he asked when we were standing under the old oak that stood in the center of my father's well-groomed backyard. I waved a hand over my head. He glanced up. "It's a treehouse."

"Yep," I said, then scurried around him to climb the boards that served as stairs. "And we're going to get jiggy in it. That *is* the term you used back in your youth, right?"

"Christ, you're a smartass," I heard him comment.

Flipping the trap door up, I shimmied through the opening, which had gotten much smaller since I was ten, eyed the low ceiling, then wiggled aside so Mads could try to get in. His shoulders almost stopped the whole secret tryst thing, but we wiggled him free and up into the cobwebby little box with windows.

"I remember this place being bigger," I mumbled while using my flashlight app to check out the place. The old Marvel posters still hung on the wall. As did one of Wayne Gretzky. "And not nearly as cold."

"And you expect us to do what in here, exactly?" Mads asked. I doused the light and crawled over to where he was seated beside one of two windows.

"I told you. We're going to sneak in a screw," I replied as I began peeling my clothes off. "Shit," I shivered when I was nude. "I'm going to freeze my nuts off."

"We can just go back inside and get back into our warm beds and fuck when we get home," he stated, but his hands felt all kinds of into the sex thing when I slithered over his lap and sat on his thighs. He was all touchy feely, his fingers roaming over my chest and shoulders as a lone beam of moonlight peeked through the window, throwing Mads and me into dappled ivory light.

"Or we can stay here and fuck now," I moaned when his touch traveled downward, his rough fingers gliding over the head of my cock.

I rocked against him, linking my fingers behind his head. He rolled his hips upward. I smiled at the hard length of him sliding up against my ass. I lowered my head, my mouth traveling over his rough cheek to his lips. He thrust his tongue in roughly, tangling it with mine as he gave me one long, hard stroke. Oh yeah, he was into this big time. His kiss was aggressive, demanding, exhilarating.

"Did you bring stuff?" Jared panted after leaving my mouth to chew on my neck like a playful tiger cub.

"What kind of tryst master would I be if I didn't bring stuff?" I asked while reaching for my hoodie.

I got his cock out of his sweats, then made fast work of the condom and lube so I could get myself seated on him properly. Knees tight to his hips, fingers locked behind his head, his hands on my hips, I eased myself down onto him. The burn and stretch stole my breath.

"Easy, go easy. Slow. Damn it, Ten. Just... shit, damn it."

I chuckled at his loss of words. I would have said something, but; I was struggling with my words too. Instead of talking, I just moved. That seemed to be the best reply. Long, slow, circular rotations of my hips that got him deeper and deeper and deeper still...

His fingers bit into my hips. With each roll of my pelvis, his cock bumped my prostate. Each bump pulled a groan from me. Each groan of mine got a matching moan from him. It was a fast, heated coupling. I came with no other stimulation than him being inside me. Mads ground his hips up into me as I rode out my orgasm, his grip almost painful. One huge thrust upward sent him over the edge as well. With his cock kicking inside me, I covered his mouth with mine, sucking on his tongue as he bucked underneath me.

I collapsed into him, my lips moving across his cheek to his neck. "God, that was epic," I murmured over his jugular. He continued to keep me in place, his fingers still firm on my hips.

"Have I told you today that I love you?" he asked, his voice thick with passion.

"Several times on the sly." I mouthed at his throat, nipping at the cords, kissing along his jaw, shuddering at the rasp of his whiskers on my tongue. I cupped his face, tipped his head, and kissed him slowly and thoroughly.

"Ten, you need to get up, babe."

"I know." I could feel him growing flaccid. I stole one more kiss, a light one, then eased myself off. Both of us made a noise of loss. "Okay, this place is a fucking freezer. What the shit is wrong with the weather?"

I scurried around searching for my clothes. When I found them, I stood up to get my pants on and nearly knocked myself unconscious. I dropped to my knees, my sleep pants around my ankles, holding the top of my head.

"Ah, fucking shit balls! Fuck! Damn this fucking hobbit house! Motherfucking horse-cocked prick ceiling! Am I bleeding? Bitch bastard *whoreson*! Who makes a roof so fucking close to the floor?! Jesus Christ on a motherfucking Zamboni!"

"Wow, you really *are* a hockey player," Mads chortled from the right. "Do we need to get you into the quiet room for concussion protocol?"

"Suck my dick, that hurt."

He laughed. "So I gathered."

I found no humor in a busted skull, but Mads was still chuckling as we climbed down from the treehouse a few minutes later. I skipped the last board and jumped to the lawn, ready to throw a scathing comment up at my lover until I heard the sliding doors from the music room opening. I whirled around. Brady and Lisa were standing two feet away from us in their pajamas, looking damn guilty. My brother was holding a couple of bed pillows, and his wife had a balled-up blanket under her arm. Her gaze flickered wildly between Mads and me as she did some quick math. Had Brady not told her about me and Mads? Going by the stupefied look on her pretty face, no he had not.

"Wow, so this isn't awkward or anything," I mumbled when Mads stepped up beside me. Four adults stood in the yard, in their sleep clothes, muttering for a moment. "Okay, so, yeah, we're going in. Have fun."

I ran to the door. Mads was chuckling even harder now. We stumbled into the kitchen snickering like Beavis and Butthead.

"Did you see the look on Lisa's face?" I snorted as I rounded the kitchen table. Mads was shutting the door as quietly as he could. "She totally did not expect to see you and me coming out of the tree house!"

"I'll admit that I was a little surprised myself," my mother said from over at the sink.

I spun to face her lurking in the darkness. Mads made a raspy choking sound. She flipped on the little light over the sink and scoured the shadows.

"Would you care to explain this, Jared?"

My jaw hit my chest. Why was she singling out Mads?

Mads cleared his throat and took a couple of steps until he could grab the back of one of the kitchen chairs. I stood by the fridge catching flies.

"It's exactly what you think it is, Jean." His gaze moved to me for a moment. Oh man, he was not as coolly calm as he wanted us to think he was. I was getting to know him well. I could see the turmoil in those stunning eyes of his. "Tennant and I are lovers."

Mom's mouth flattened. She glanced at me. "How long have you and Jared been a couple?"

"Define being a couple," I said.

Her flat mouth puckered. Yep. I'd stepped right into it. Even Mads grunted at the remark.

"You know full well what being a couple means, Tennant. Were you and Jared lovers when you told your father and I that you were gay?"

"We hadn't really—"

Mads shouldered his way into the conversation. "Yes, Jean, we were."

"Thank you for being a mature adult and answering my question respectfully, Jared."

Ow. Ouch. That one hurt like a puck to the groin.

"We should have told you and Bruce weeks ago. I take full responsibility for that. I should have come to you and Bruce before Ten and I started dating and sat down with you."

"Really, Mads? What is this, the fourteenth century? Asking my parents if we can see each other? Uh, no. I make that call, not them."

"Tennant, this is not the time to get your ass up," Jared said tersely.

"Do you know what hurts me the most, Tennant?" Mom sliced into the snipe-fest between me and my boyfriend. I pulled my gaze away from Mads. "It's not that you and him snuck out to diddle around in the tree house. Brady and Jamie have been using that damn old thing for sneaking sex when they stay here for years."

And I'd thought I was being so sneaky clever. "I didn't want to do that in your house," I told her weakly.

The confession didn't seem to make her less angry… or hurt. Her arms were wound around her middle as if I'd gut-punched her and she was expecting another one.

"Your father and I are well aware that our sons aren't leading celibate lives." She stopped protecting her middle to fold her arms over her chest. "But I do appreciate that you have respect enough for us to take your romping to the tree house. See, it's not that I'm mad that you and Jared snuck out to fool around, and I'm not even mad that you've chosen Jared as a lover. He's a good man who's been a friend of this family for years. That he's slightly older is a good thing. He'll temper how rash you can be at times."

Rash? I wasn't rash. Was I? What did that mean exactly? I wished I could Google it, but it really wasn't the time. "What I'm upset about is that you—out of all my boys—*you* hid this relationship from me even after you came out."

"I know. I'm sorry. I just… Coming out was drama enough, you know? I couldn't… It's not that I didn't want to tell you, Mom."

"Do your brothers know?"

Mads shuffled a bit beside me, the chair creaking as he pushed down on the back a little harder. If he broke it, Mom would whip us both with the broken spindles.

"Tennant, look at me," she said.

I had to now, but I so didn't want to. Her gaze met mine. I nodded. Mom inhaled, coughed a little, and squared her shoulders.

"Brady walked in on us after we'd been…" I let the explanation wither.

"And I thought we were so close." She pulled her robe tightly around her and walked out, leaving a soft cloud of her flowery perfume behind. I moved to follow her. Mads grabbed my shoulder, turning me around to face him.

"Let her be for a bit, Ten. She's feeling abandoned. I get that. If Ryker had someone in his life that he was sleeping with, I'd like to think he'd tell me about her… or him."

"But I was *going* to tell them. Shit. Man, this is fucked."

Jared pulled me to his chest and curled his arms around me. I sank into his embrace. This was not at *all* how this visit home was supposed to be playing out.

RASH. It's an adjective. It means "displaying or proceeding from a lack of careful consideration of the possible consequences of an action." Mom said that I was rash. That meant she thought I was reckless or something. I pulled back the curtains on my bedroom window as the sun started to touch the sky with hot, pink fingers. When had I ever been reckless? Sure, I guess one could say that hooking up with my coach was a little impulsive, but love happens. We don't have any control over who we fall for. Ugh. I threw the curtain back into place and sat on the edge of my bed. The bed that I had not slept in. Who the hell could sleep after ripping out their mother's heart? Mads was probably pulling some big T & Ts—tossing and turnings—down in the basement as Ryker sawed wood beside him on the pullout. I wished I was beside him right now. Maybe he'd have some wise words for me. He was rugged and tough and travel worn. Shit. I'd just described my grandmother's luggage.

Knowing I was never going to sleep unless I fixed things with my mother, I went in search of her. I found Dad instead, making coffee while listening to some old seventies music on his iPad. He gave me a disappointed look over the shoulder of his favorite robe as it dangled off his arm. Dad woke up slowly.

"Is Mom up?" I enquired, dropping into what had been Jamie's chair when we were all home. I picked up the chicken-shaped salt shaker to examine it.

"She is, but she's resting for a little longer. She has a busy day today."

I peeked from the salt shaker to Dad as he poured water into the back of the coffee maker. "Did she tell you about things?"

My gaze went back to the glass hen in my palm. She

was a cute chicken. White with black dots and a yellow beak.

"Yes, she did. Tennant, why don't you put that down and look at me?"

"Because I didn't let this chicken down." I sighed, but placed the hen next to the rooster. The napkin holder was empty, I noticed.

"You didn't let your mother down either."

"Pft. Right."

He shuffled over, put a hand on my Pokémon tattoo, and squeezed hard. "You didn't let anyone down. She realizes that. Why don't you go fiddle around in the music room until the coffee's done? Then we can talk more if she's not down yet."

"Okay, yeah." I pushed out of my seat, shoulders sagging.

The music room was always the first to feel the touch of the sun. I plunked my sorry ass on the long bench in front of the massive black Steinway. For some reason that room was warmer than the rest of the house. Mom said it was because music warmed a soul better than any old forced air unit ever could. The sun peeked around the oak that cradled our treehouse. I poked at a couple of keys, then flipped through the sheet music on the rack. Holiday songs. Mom loved her Christmas carols. She'd been probably playing for the girls. I felt like the biggest bag of dicks in the world. Pulling one of the sheets out of the middle, I studied the notes and decided I could play it. Maybe.

I got halfway through "The Dance of the Cygnets" from "The Nutcracker," then faltered. Tried again and nailed it. Then I moved into "The Dance of the Sugar Plum Fairy" as the sun hit the ebony piano and the side of my face.

"Nicely done, but your fingers were drooping." Mom

sat down beside me, her tiny butt taking little room. The last notes I'd played danced on the air to join the dust motes frolicking about in that fat ray of sun washing over us.

"Mom…"

"No, Tennant, you did nothing wrong." She wiggled her hip a bit. I scooted over a couple of inches, then peeked to the side.

Her hair was all brushed, her lipstick on, and her robe neatly tied over her pajamas. Just like every holiday morning I could recall. Except the holiday mornings of the past hadn't included me being gay and having Mads as a lover. Man, things had been way easier back then.

"It was me." She exhaled loudly, then glanced at me. "I'm a foolish woman at times. How dare I expect you to tell me every damn thing in your life now that you're an adult just because you used to when you were five?"

"Mom, I *swear* I was going to tell you and Dad today… somehow."

She patted my thigh, then picked a black lab hair from my jogging pants. That too floated off to join the notes and dust motes.

"You know what? Even if you hadn't told us today, that would have been okay. It's not for me to say when you fill me in on who you're taking to bed. My God, I'm so nosy! It's terrible." She sort of laughed at herself.

I smiled a little. "See, the thing was that I wasn't even sure what Mads and I were then, you know? I mean, we were crazy attracted to each other but… man, this is hard." I shoved my hands through my hair. Mom instantly reached up to flatten the mess back down. That made me feel lighter inside.

"I just needed time. *We* needed time. To figure it out, to make sure. There's been so much shit—I mean stuff—

going on in our lives since I went to Harrisburg. I never meant for Brady to be the first to know, he just kind of showed up at Mads' when I was there wearing strawberries and… You know what, we won't go there, but if I could have picked one person to tell face to face, it would have been you."

"You're a sweet young man, Tennant. I hope Jared knows how lucky he is." She kissed me on the cheek, then reached up to pull out another sheet filled with notes. "How about one more song before I have to start baking pies and stuffing the turkey?"

"Sure, you pick."

I knew before I saw the sheet music what it would be. Her favorite song by her favorite Piano Man. Not Christmas or Thanksgiving related at all, but it felt right. I played and we sang. When we got to the part about Levon being a good man, she reached up to grab my chin and sing those words right at me. Mom and I rocked that song to the very end. I gave her a soft kiss on the cheek and went off to find Mads. He was just coming up the stairs with Ryker on his heels.

"My mom says you're a lucky man," I told him as I wrapped my arms around him.

"I know that," he murmured, before accepting the long, hard kiss I gave him in front of God and my half-awake family.

The rest of the day was off-the-charts good. Tons of food, football, and cuddles on the couch with Mads. I shit you not. Mads and I. On the couch. Cuddling like a couple. And no one was freaked out in the least. After the meal was done at four, Ryker sat on one side of Mads and I on the other. The women folk were in the kitchen cleaning up. We manly men were spread out trying to digest and not fall asleep while we made predictions on who would win the Vikings–Lions matchup. My head was lolling on Mads' shoulder as I battled off a nap. The tones of a mobile Pokémon game danced into my sleepy ears.

"Ryker, what does it mean when this happens?" I heard Mads whisper.

I rolled my head to the left to find Mads showing his son his morphing Pokémon creature.

"*Dude*, are you evolving your Charmander?!" I asked, all sleepiness burning off. Jamie was snoring in the recliner.

"Maybe," Mads replied with a wicked smile toying at his kissable mouth.

"Okay, I love you more than pumpkin pie. I want to have your baby." I grabbed his face and kissed him loudly. "Guys, we're going to go make a baby. Be back in twenty minutes," I told my brothers, father, and the dog. Bourque woofed lazily.

"Better give us thirty," Mads tossed out, but couldn't move due to overconsumption of turkey, stuffing, green bean casserole, and mashed potatoes with gravy.

"You can have one of mine. Lisa made a spare," Brady said around a yawn.

"Maybe we should digest a little more before we try to make a baby," Mads offered, and yawned as well.

"Good call." I curled into his side, sighed like a cat filled with cream, and promptly fell asleep.

It sucked having to leave that evening, but all of us had games either the next day or Saturday. Ryker dozed on the flight back, his head resting on the window, his dad's Railers coaching jacket as a pillow. Jared sat between his son and me, reading a book, his strong, masculine profile keeping me mesmerized. When he felt me staring, he glanced up from his book—some old thing with a knight on the front—and gave me a questioning look as he placed his open book on his thigh.

"You're really handsome," I said with a smile.

His gaze flickered to the people sitting in front of us, as if he were worried that they'd hear me saying that. With the love of a good family and this man welling up inside me, I placed my hand over his and his book.

"Ten, are you sure you want to make such a public gesture?" he asked softly.

I threaded my fingers through his. "I've never been more positive of anything in my life."

He lifted my knuckles to his lips. "I'll be right beside you."

I sat back in my seat, my fingers woven with his, and let my eyes drift closed. If I had Mads with me I could face anything my coming out publicly would bring. I'd have to. There was no way I wanted to go back to hiding us from the world. Maybe after I made the announcement I could just go back to playing hockey and loving Jared Madsen. You know… the important things in life.

Epilogue

MADS

Ten couldn't sit still, he fidgeted and fussed with the hem of his jersey and even though I placed a steadying hand on his knee he couldn't stop. Not that I was any better. This was big, enormous, life changing stuff and it all hinged on a yes from both of us.

"The concept of being the first out hockey player isn't a small thing," Ten said, and he placed a hand over mine and gripped hard.

"Which is why we're bringing in a crisis management expert. This is non-negotiable Ten, how we deal with this as a team will inform one hell of a lot of future decisions. For the team, and for hockey."

All I could think of was the kid out there on the ice somewhere in the ass end of Canada, worried about being honest with himself and everyone else for fear of not being able to play. I didn't care, I was out, but I could be out, I was an *ex player*. Also, the bi thing meant that the label of gay wasn't one that was used to describe me.

But Ten? He'd be Tennant Rowe, the openly gay player for the Railers...

When you played you didn't hear the shit that the opposing teams threw at you, but what if that shit was coming from your team supporters? What if Ten coming out drove away crowds or became the subject of hate crimes. He'd said last night he wasn't sure he was ready to be the person with millions of words of hate thrown at him. I could have said that it didn't matter, but both of us knew it did.

The week since Thanksgiving had been stressful, but weirdly also calm. Ten was internalizing a lot of this, and I didn't need to have attended therapy to know that.

"Ten?" I asked.

Ten looked at me, and gripped my hand tight. "Okay," he said. "Let's do this."

Coach opened the door and a man in a suit strode in. He exuded confidence and honesty in equal measures. He seemed to be a settled in his own skin, pretty much how I was now. All we needed for Ten was to get him to that point as well.

He extended a hand. "Layton Foxx," he said, and smiled as he spoke. "I am so pleased to meet you Mr. Rowe, Mr. Madsen."

"Mads," I corrected.

"Ten," Ten said at the same time.

We exchanged smiles, Mads and Ten could take on the world. Together.

Layton sat down. "Okay," he began, "so this is what we propose."

I listened to the words, heard every one of them, I think.

But all I could really focus on was Ten's hand in mine, and enjoy the fact that I was loved, and in love, and that together we could beat anything that was thrown at us.

Anything at all.

. . .

THE END

Next for the Railers

First Season (Harrisburg Railers Hockey #2)

Layton wants success, Adler wants family, how can love make both these things possible?

Layton Foxx works hard for what he has. The condo, the career, the chance to make his mark, is all down to the sacrifices he has made. With tragedy in his past, he doesn't want or need love. Then he meets Adler Lockhart, the extroverted, sexy winger for the Harrisburg Railers and abruptly he can't avoid love even if he wanted to.

Adler Lockhart has had everything handed to him his whole life. Cars, villas, cash, college tuition at the finest Ivy League schools. The only things he doesn't have are parents who care or the love of a good man. Then Layton walks into his privileged life and shows him what real love can be like.

Hockey Series' from RJ Scott & V.L. Locey

Harrisburg Railers

Owatonna U Hockey

Arizona Raptors

Boston Rebels

LA Storm

Chesterford Coyotes - Young Adult

Free Reads

Please note - in all of these free stories, there will be some spoilers for the main series books.

Railers Short Stories

Volume 1 | Volume 2

LA Storm

Sparkle

The Colts - AHL Short Stories

Pucks & Percentages

Breakaway

Making the Save

Standalone

Waiting for Christmas

Harrisburg Railers

When hockey wunderkind Tennant Rowe meets his new coach, he knows he's in trouble. Jared Madsen is nine years older than Tennant, impossibly attractive, and — worst of all — his brother's off-limits best friend. Is their chemistry worth the risk?

Changing Lines (Railers 1)

Can Tennant show Jared that age is just a number, and that love is all that matters?

The Rowe Brothers are famous hockey hotshots, but as the youngest of the trio, Tennant has always had to play against his brothers' reputations. To get out of their shadows, and against their advice, he accepts a trade to the Harrisburg Railers, where he runs into Jared Madsen. Mads is an old family friend and his brother's one-time teammate. Mads is Tennant's new coach. And Mads is the sexiest thing he's ever laid eyes on.

Jared Madsen's hockey career was cut short by a fault in his heart, but coaching keeps him close to the game. When Ten is traded to the team, his carefully organized world is thrown into chaos. Nine years his junior and his best friend's brother, he knows Ten is strictly off-limits, but as soon as he sees Ten's moves, on and off the ice, he knows that his heart could get him into trouble again.

Changing Lines

Harrisburg Railers (Hockey Romance)

1. Changing Lines
2. First Season
3. Deep Edge
4. Poke Check
5. Last Defense
6. Goal Line
7. Neutral Zone
8. Hat Trick
9. Save The Date
10. Baby Makes Three
11. Rivals
12. Perfect Gifts
13. Family First

Railers Volume 1 | Railers Volume 2 | Railers Volume 3 | Railers Volume 4

Meet the men of Owatonna University's hockey team

Ryker (Owatonna U, 1)

Ryker

Ryker is hockey royalty, Jacob is a poor country boy. Can two vastly different people find common ground and become the men they want to be?

Ryker comes from a long line of championship-winning hockey players. Playing college hockey to develop his game is his only focus, and nothing will stand in the way of him working to become the best player. He has no room for relationships, people who point out his flaws, or anyone who calls him on his dreams. He certainly has no place for love, and meeting Jacob is nothing but a useful distraction on the side. After all trying to get his Owatonna Eagles teammate into bed is less work and more play. When tragedy rocks his family, his charmed life crumbles, and the only person he can turn to is the same one who claims to hate him.

Jacob Benson has only known hard work and stifling conservative values his whole life. Born and raised in the small rural community of Eden Crossing, Minnesota, he's the only son of a hard-working but struggling dairy farming family. Jacob is using his skills in hockey to finance his way to an agricultural science degree. These four years at Owatonna U. will probably be the only time he has to enjoy life, gain acceptance about his sexuality, and live openly before his inevitable return to the farm. Running into a pretty rich boy like Ryker Madsen is putting a damper on his enjoyment of life away from home. Ryker's flip, conceited, carefree attitude grates on Jacob's every nerve. So why, if Ryker is everything he dislikes, does he want nothing more than to explore the sinful dreams that his annoying teammate stars in every night?

Ryker

Owatonna U Hockey (Hockey Romance)

Coast to Coast (Arizona Raptors 1)

Coast To Coast

When opposites attract, this bottom-of-the-league team will never be the same again.

A stipulation in his father's will forces Mark back into the arms of a family that disowned him and leaves him one-third owner of a hockey team facing financial ruin. He doesn't even watch hockey, let alone like it, and wants nothing more than to head back to New York. Then there's the new coach, a stubborn, opinionated, irritating man with superiority issues and questionable music taste. Butting heads with Rowen becomes the new normal, but it comes with passionate debate and an all-consuming lust.

Challenged to rebuild one of the worst teams in the league into a future cup contender, Rowen can't pass up the opportunity. Never in his twenty years of hockey has he ever seen a team managed so badly or coached players overflowing with resentment and bigotry. Yet there's something about this team and this city that compels him to roll up his sleeves and start dismantling. If only Mark, one of three siblings who now own the Raptors, wasn't so damned rock-headed yet so damned appealing his job might be easier. It doesn't look like either is willing to give in, but one night in a dark, desert hotel changes everything.

Coast To Coast

Arizona Raptors (Hockey Romance)

1. Coast To Coast
2. Across the Pond
3. Shadow and Light
4. Sugar and Ice
5. School and Rock

Top Shelf (Boston Rebels 1)

Acting on the attraction to his best friend's brother has always been off the table for Xander until a passionate hookup with Mason at a beach resort begins a love affair that burns long after summer ends.

Mason specializes in assisting same-sex couples on their journey to becoming parents and fighting every rule that blocks his way in the stuck-in-the-past agency that hired him. Living in his brother's pool house is rent-free, and every cent he earns he saves for his dream—that one day he'd have his own company helping others. The downside is that he has to see his annoying brother every day, the upside is that his brother's teammates from the Boston Rebels make regular visits. The eye candy that passes Mason's window is almost enough to make him consider dating a hockey player, but not just any player though. Ever since Xander —his brother's childhood friend—came out as gay at a press conference, Mason's puppy love has turned into a burning attraction he can no longer ignore.

Hockey has been one of Xander's main focuses since he was old enough to balance on skates. Well, hockey and Mason Kingsley, but Mason was always unattainable. Now that he's about to see thirty candles on his birthday cake and is no longer hiding the fact he's gay, he's ready to find a soul mate to make his life complete. A summer vacation is just what he needs to have time to think, but when the Boston Rebels arriving in paradise with Mason in tow, thinking is the last thing he needs. One torrid night under a balmy moon and rules about not messing with his best friend's brother vanish on a warm, tropical breeze.

Summer romances don't generally last past Labor Day, but with the new season about to begin Xander and Mason are going to have to face the world and decide if their love is real enough to withstand everything.

Boston Rebels

Lost In Boston (Free Prequel Novella)

1. Top Shelf
2. Back Check
3. Snowed
4. Royal Lines
5. Blade
6. Rental

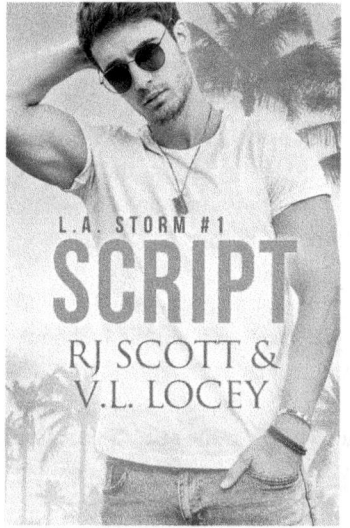

Script (LA Storm, 1)

Script

Hollywood A-lister Finn might be Canadian, but he needs Cameron to show him how to hockey.

Actor Finn Kerrigan is at a crossroads. After growing up a soap star, then starring in a hugely successful trilogy of action movies, he's finally given the chance to read a heartfelt and passionate script that could change his life forever. The role would be enough for people to see him as a serious actor, and maybe even win him an award or two (and no, a golden raspberry award for his action movies doesn't count). Once established as a serious actor he's sure he can come out of the closet and finally live his truth. When he lies to get the part of a hockey player on a struggling team, he suddenly has nowhere to hide. He might be Canadian, but the last time he skated he was ten, and no, he doesn't have hockey in his blood. With only a month until filming starts, he about to be exposed, but partnered with a player who's supposed to be giving him tips, he doesn't realize how many of his secrets will come to light. Falling in lust, one heated kiss at a time, is inevitable, but giving Cameron up at the end of the shoot could break his heart.

Cameron Chavkin is the face of the LA Storm. And the body, and the hair, and the smile. He's at the prime of his career, men and women want to be with him, and he's skating better than he ever has before. His house sits next to a famous rock star's mansion, his garage is filled with expensive cars, and he's even been asked to mentor a once-famous actor in a new hockey movie. Life is pretty sweet. Until the bad boy of hockey meets Finn, a man on the edge with more secrets than Cameron has endorsements. Knowing better than to get involved, Cameron is swept up despite himself, and when it's time to say goodbye to the Storm's most eligible bachelor is finding it hard to follow the script.

Script

LA Storm

Off The Ice (Chesterford Coyotes, 1)

Off The Ice

A coming-of-age love story with high school, hockey rivalry, friendship, family, and coming out.

Soren's life changes in an instant when he and his younger brother are adopted by hockey royalty. Making sense of his new life is hard enough, but when he's enrolled in a private school it means facing a whole new set of problems. Navigating friendship, family, and hockey is one thing, but being attracted to the boy who vexes him is a whole new thing.

Felix has a reputation to protect. He's the kid who seems to have everything but looks can be deceiving. Spinning lies about his perfect life, he's created a fantasy world that even he has started to believe. Only, it's not long before everything crumbles, all of his pretty lies are revealed, and only his closest rival sees through his pain and stands by him.

Fighting is easy, friendship is hard, but love is everything.

Off The Ice

Chesterford Coyotes

1. Off The Ice
2. On Thin Ice
3. *Dance on Ice*

Also By RJ Scott

For a full list of ebooks and links please scan the code above or
visit rjscott.co.uk/rjbooks

Meet RJ Scott

RJ discovered romance in books at a very young age and realized that if there wasn't romance on the page, she could create it in her head. With over one hundred and fifty books published, she is a full time author of gay romance.

She lives and works out of her home in the beautiful English countryside, spends her spare time reading, watching films, and enjoying time with her family.

The last time she had a week's break from writing she didn't like it one little bit and has yet to meet a box of chocolates she couldn't defeat.

www.rjscott.co.uk | rj@rjscott.co.uk

NEWSLETTER - rjscott.co.uk/rjnews

facebook.com/author.rjscott

x.com/Rjscott_author

instagram.com/rjscott_author

amazon.com/author/rj-scott

bookbub.com/authors/rj-scott

goodreads.com/rjscott

pinterest.com/rjscottauthor

Also By VL Locey

For a full list of ebooks and links please scan the code above or
visit vllocey.com/stories-from-vl-locey

Meet V.L. Locey

V.L. Locey loves worn jeans, yoga, belly laughs, walking, reading and writing lusty tales, Greek mythology, the New York Rangers, comic books, and coffee.

(Not necessarily in that order.)

She shares her life with her husband, her daughter, one dog, two cats, a flock of assorted domestic fowl, and two Jersey steers.

When not writing spicy romances, she enjoys spending her day with her menagerie in the rolling hills of Pennsylvania with a cup of fresh java in hand.

vllocey.com
vicki@vllocey.com

Newsletter - vllocey.com/newsletter

f facebook.com/V.L.Locey

X x.com/vllocey

instagram.com/vl_locey

BB bookbub.com/authors/v-l-locey

g goodreads.com/vllocey

pinterest.com/vllocey